ULDERELM

A UNIVERSE OF DARKNESS NOVEL
ADVENTURE TWO

ULDERELM

A UNIVERSE OF DARKNESS NOVEL
ADVENTURE TWO

Timothy Alan. Milam Jr.

Amazon / Kindle publishing

ULDERELM
**A UNIVERSE OF DARKNESS NOVEL
ADVENTURE TWO**

Timothy Alan Milam Jr.

Amazon / Kindle publishing

This is a work of fiction. All the characters, events and directions within this novella are products of the author's imagination.

ULDERELM

Printed in the USA.

This second chapter to A Universe of Darkness is dedicated to all my fans that have fallen in love with the world of Buriece and are excited to visit a whole new world. Thanks for the support. Enjoy.

The Broken Seal

A blaze ignited, manifesting into the darkness, and stood upon the mountain pass that overlooked Hazu. It was a small village that was headed by one of five keepers, to the keys of silence. The elder was not there that night for he was out on duties with another town, to secure rations, for their supplies were thin.

The inferno burned white hot as it made its way through the village. The fire could taste the key, like it was calling out to it, summoning it.

Each grass hut it passed caught fire and instantly went up in flames. Screams erupted from within the dancing orange glow. Some were fortunate to escape, while others were prisoners to the chaotic energy.

Smoke billowed from the village as it went down in flames. The people who had gotten out in time began trying to extinguish the fire from the nearby river. Their efforts were futile for the fire was eternal and would never be stubbed out, not to mention the river was a good distance at a fast run.

The protectors of the key of silence who were dormant for the past three thousand years had been awakened. They stirred within the confines of their chamber waiting for the threat to knock upon their keep.

The power inside them came alive and sparked a fight, a hunger to protect the key of silence. The last time they were called upon they were at full strength from the energy of the sun. This day, three thousand years later their strength would be no match for the blaze that terrorizes Hazu, since the arrival of the purple haze, the darkness that blocked out the sun.

The entrance to the protector's lair was a

large circular gate made of ancient metal, which was charmed by the elders as an extra precaution to keep the weather from getting in.

The dark core within the inferno hissed and cracked as the flames engulfed it. One fiery hand lashed out at the gate. The dark power that the fire pixie had was at full strength and was stronger than the forces that keep the gate sealed and since the arrival of the darkness, it will prove even stronger then the protectors.

The gate exploded, sending shrapnel flying. The fire pixie entered the three-thousand-year-old prison and descended the man-made steps, the dust kicked up by the breeze began to spark as the flames from the creature licked it.

Down in the keep the protectors waited. They could feel the entity drawing nearer. The power emanating from it was fierce and they knew they were no match for it and they did what they were made to do in case they could not protect the key of silence. They were going to fight but they knew their life would be consumed the fire element.

They used the last amount of their power and summoned a warning. A warning that would call out to one of the elders of silence. The one that was chosen to receive the warning.

The roar of the fire echoed throughout the keep as it ascended upon the protectors and began to annihilate them.

Elders of Silence

Elkron froze in mid-flight. A sickening feeling that he never thought would happen was signaling a warning inside of his head. It meant that one of the five keys of silence were no longer safe, and he now needed to alert the other elders more than ever.

He flew to mount Arion as quickly as he could, which was not a short journey. It took him three full days in the shittiest weather imaginable. Not to mention the darkness that now covered the land, which was his main reason for traveling to mount Arion in the first place but now it seems his destiny has been set in motion.

He was glad he had just finished foraging

before he was summoned. It would seem the creator had planned things out accordingly.

He had to finish his journey on foot because the altitude was too high for him to fly. It was a total of ten miles through waist high snow, that he had to travel and by the time he made it to the summit he wanted to kill over. He was grateful for the rock cabin that awaited him, where it stood for three thousand years, just as he and the other elders had built it. Except now it was covered in a thick blanket of snow and was almost hidden.

The Horn of Sorrow sat at the edge of the summit barely visible in the snow that covered it. It was a rare, one of a kind instrument made from the blood of the innocent, the blood of children.

The day it was forged was a day that he nor the other elders would never forget because that was the day they were the villains. The day they were evil. He could still see their faces. The innocent children's faces. It was all for peace, to help the future. The future that was now. They knew the time would come and here it was.

The elders murdered over two thousand children that day as a sacrifice for Ulderelm. They needed enough innocent blood to obtain the minerals within it to forge the Horn of Sorrows.

The blood had to be innocent or the power would not work. The innocence was children. He and the elders had no choice or, so they believed, but that was a mental struggle he's lived with for three thousand years and has tried to justify it as a just cause but that was a deception. No matter how they chalked it up, it was still morally wrong.

Elkron looked out over Ulderelm and even with the darkness, he could see the fires from Mount Fire and it looked as imposing from this distance as it did up close. More than three hundred miles from where he was, the trails of fire that ran down its surface were visible.

He wiped the snow from the mouth of the

horn and then went to the front and cleared out the bell and with raised wings in the air he took in a deep breath. The cold air burned as it filled his lungs and then he placed his chapped lips to the mouth of the Horn of Sorrow and blew into it. The Horn came to life.

The sound of over two thousand innocent children were awakened. Their cries echoed loudly, out into the lands beyond. The eerie sound was sure to frighten the world but call to the elders, to tell them that it was time to gather.

Once the chilling sound came to an end, he went to the cabin. Now, he rested to regain his strength for the long journey that awaited him. It was only part over.

Next, he would be meeting the other elders in the Shallows. A dead wasteland, none would travel for the fear of never returning and for good reason, and that reason was because it was so close to Mount Fire. They used the Shallows as a place to conjure the creator, to gain his guidance. To gain information into the world in which they live.

The next morning before the land got bright but not by much, Elkron set out on his long journey West. He figured he would be the last elder to arrive. None of them had ever hoped to see each other again after that day on Mount Arion. After all the time that has passed they had thought they never would but now he summoned them, and the union would be very unpleasant, he expected. Informative, but unpleasant.

Once he got low enough down the mountain, he took to the sky. He beat his wings and pushed through the air. It was a relief to finally be free of struggling in the snow and now time was now too precious to waste and whatever was happening was progressing faster than the elders had predicted.

One key was in the enemy's hands and he was still days away. He knew not, how long before the next four keys were in danger, but he was sure he would hear the protector's warnings.

The protectors were created from an alloy called Greenite, which was the strongest in Ulderelm and was given the power of the sun and then infused with the elder's blood, which made them almost invincible, but it would appear not to whatever threatened them now, this day.

Once the keys are free then the Nightmare would be free and this time the world of the living would be no more. When Thondrous fulfilled his destiny long ago by locking the Nightmare in a prison of light, Thondrous burst into the five keys of silence.

The elders were then in charge of hiding the keys and once they had successfully fulfilled their quest; the five elders were stripped of their voices, to better keep the keys of silence a secret.

Elkron wondered if the creator would again make a new hero, such as Thondrous in this dire time and he could see no reason as to why he would not, with the purple new haze that has now shadowed the land. He also wondered what new threat has come upon their world. Soon enough he will find out... Maybe.

He would also hope to find out which key had been threatened and hopefully not stolen and he hoped it was not the one he had hidden in his tiny village of Fihlar, which was in the far Northwest part of Ulderelm, while he was on his way to call forth the other elders but he had no time to check the status of his little farming village, so he would have to hope for the best.

Since the haze has arrived, it was difficult to tell what part of the day it truly was. Especially if it was an overcast day, which was rare for Ulderelm, since it was mostly, always sunny.

When he had left Arion, it would have been an hour or more before the sun would have risen and as far as he could tell it was a clear day. That was until he got out of the mountain range and to the outskirts of Gredge and the neighboring swamp lands; for it was now overcast and raining. He figured it had to be about noon or so, guessing by the contrast of the darkness.

Another hour or so and he would be to Gredge. A small village that was known mostly for their herbal remedies and many desperate people and creatures, would travel from far away to seek out the cures that they might have, but those travelers would need a very heavy coin to get what they wanted.

Out in the distance the little town looked dark and foreboding from the haze. He flew past and into the swamplands, which looked equally as unpleasant as Gredge did. He supposed Ulderelm was going to be this way for some time but hopefully not forever.

Night had come he figured because it was now much darker up in the clouds then before and he needed to press on, but he was far too tired to go on any further, from trying to save time by flying faster to cover more ground. Now he found himself in a dilemma and had not thought much about it, since his mind was on much pressing matters and that was sleep and it had slipped his mind until now and he was in the middle of nowhere.

After passing Gredge and the swamplands, he had decided to take a shortcut, since he knew which direction he needed to go but it was completely without life for miles.

He did however see a group of Molgren's, which was very rare, this far Northeast. What they were doing this far from their territory around Mount Fire was a mystery but Elkron knew that it could not be good.

The Molgren's were a large hairy beast with razor sharp teeth and glowing red eyes and were said to be a cursed race of humans.

They hung in large colonies and moved like the wind. If a being came face to face with one, their lives were finished. They could strip a creature to the bone in less than a minute. They were a nocturnal beast, but it seems that this dark haze has brought them out whenever they pleased, which would be a major problem.

It was said that long ago when the world was new the Molgren's lived at the base of Mount Fire and that they were a normal tribe of people and one day a man came, but he wasn't really a man but a man with powers, which was far from normal for humans and he took over the tribe, demanding that they worship him. The Molgren's were forced to pay their loyalties with gold and if they could not pay, he would feed them to the lava at the top of Mount Fire. He proved this by taking one of their people, a remedy maker, the only remedy maker and held him over the mouth of the mountain with dark powers and when the people pleaded with the man with powers to free him, the man let go. A haunting, terrifying scream came as the remedy maker descended to his death.

The human that was once in charge of the tribe had had enough and challenged the powerful man to a fight. A fight to the death and when the leader asked for a fair fight, the man denied him the request. The human knew the powerful man would not forfeit his powers; so, he had to devise a plan and it had to be executed perfectly or it would not work.

The evening before the challenge the leader consulted with a few of the tribe members about the plan he had, and he was surprised that he had multiple volunteers willing to sacrifice their lives for their freedom.

Needless to say, the plan worked but not as it was intended. When the time had come to execute the plan, the volunteers stepped forward and started screaming, making the man with powers turn away from the leader.

The leader had a spear and while the man was momentarily distracted. The leader threw it straight and true. The man with great powers squeezed the throats of the ones who screamed with his powers, crushing them to death. When he turned back to face his oppressor the spear entered and exited his heart.

The whole tribe watched as the man dropped down to his knees. Everyone thought that the servitude was over. They all looked on, waiting for the man to take his last breath.

Instantly the man began speaking strange words as blood was pouring from his mouth as he spoke, clinging to the last bit of life he had left. Suddenly the whole tribe started to convulse and contort. Their skin began burning in the rays of the sun. Then course hair began pushing through their skin. Their eyes went blind as the sun sizzled them and their teeth began chipping and cracking, falling out leaving them as points.

The powerful man finally dropped dead but every one of the tribe's people, screamed in agony as the sun singed the hair that now covered their entire bodies. They all ran into the confines of their huts to escape the, now morbid sun. They have been confined to darkness ever since.

Such a story he was told long ago when he was younger. He has never heard it told again and never bothered with knowing it every again, but it's been there in his mind. How they became known as Molgren's was a mystery to him.

He wondered what kind of madness has forsaken the land now with the Molgren's running rampant. He could only imagine, but only in time will he and the other elders know most of, if not all the details of what has begun to plague the land.

Settling down for some sleep, where he had found himself a small group of trees to conceal himself in. It was not that cozy, but he didn't care. He tucked his head within the confines of his wings and drifted off.

The next morning, he woke up from an eerie sound. He slowly peeked his head out from his wings. Trying to see through the branches was difficult since they were so confined. He could see movement through narrow spaces but that was all.

He slowly climbed up to the canopy to have a better look. The sight was as eerie as the sound. He has never seen anything like it before and he has been alive a long time.

Not that far from him was a thing that was clear like water and made the images behind it, distorted. It wasn't really walking, not in the sense of a man but it was moving. It sloshed as it came in contact with the ground and a sucking noise as it pulled itself off. The transparent figure was quite large. If he had to guess, he would say that it was approximately the size of a small pond that one could easily swim inside of.

He didn't notice it before, since the background blurred the images with it, but it had a core. A small black, man size fist of a core.

He sat roosted in the top of the tree watching this strange creature, observing it. Knowing a little about it may come in helpful later on. The liquid just kept on moving North. It did not appear to oppose a threat, but he was not about to get close enough to find out.

He wanted to follow the strange liquid creature but he knew the elders were on their way and so he must be getting on his way as well. He needed answers before chaos consumed the world.

Summoning

As Elkron had assumed, he was the last of the elders to arrive at the Shallows. He glided down and landed among the other four, who looked to be in a damper mood.

"I apologize for my late arrival. I do hope you have not waited long." Elkron scribbled in the dust.

"We have only but arrived this morning or whatever part of the day it is." Sagfrin mentioned as she scraped her message in the dry ground and then tossed dust into the air, out of frustration.

Sagfrin was the only female in the group and she was the wisest of all the elders. She was the leader of Drenchin. A large prosperous city that held the world's largest population. It was more modern than the other towns, which kept themselves basic and saw no need to upgrade and it was also the center of all trade routes.

Elkron had only visited it once in his lifetime and never bothered with it again. He was more of a small village type and he preferred to deal with as few beings as possible.

"Have any of you witnessed anything strange beyond the purple haze that shrouds the land?" Elkron asked.

The four elders shook their heads, no. They waited for Elkron to finish his message in the dirt. He described the strange water creature and told them about seeing a horde of Molgren's. He went on about how one of the keys of silence has been breached and could now be in the hands of the enemy.

The four elders huffed and scrapped their feet across the ground. All four fluffed their chest feathers in a panic.

"It would appear that this darkness has brought about chaos to our world. Let us be quick to summon the creator and get further details. We must hurry to protect the living." Framen wrote in haste.

Framen was the youngest elder of the five, for he was very smart given his age and fit in well with the cause of protecting Ulderelm and its inhabitants. He was the leader of Quezen, which was the third largest city and is known for its heavy grain growth.

It was also heavily populated with Rharv's, which is a race like humans but who had horns and long mustaches, with arms that almost touched the ground and short stubby legs. Male and female didn't differ much in appearance except for their breasts and genitals. They are known as the best metal craftsmen in Ulderelm. People and creatures traveled far to seek out their skills, when needing armor, weapons and even tools.

"Yes, let us be on with it before we die out here!" Jupin scribbled. The oldest and most moody elder. Nicknamed Grumpy Jupin, which was something the other elders referred to him as but not to his face.

He was leader of Hazu, a very small village that was smaller than Elkron's. It sat below the far southern mountain, Elmrose and wasn't visited very often, since it was so far off the trade routes and they really didn't have much to offer the world, except perhaps a view.

The last elder said nothing, he just observed everything, which was his thing and has been, even before they were stripped of their vocals.

His name was Piko and he was from the forest town of Clavindar that was deep in the Clavin forest, which was home to a race called the Arglar, who were a feminine tree dwelling creature, with very fine hairs from head to toe and that never left the confines of the forest and are said to never age. Piko claimed they were a very peaceful creature.

The Clavin forest was thick and dangerous, especially at night. Even in the day, a traveler still had to be well aware of their surroundings, so they would not be robbed or killed. Although the forest was dangerous, Clavindar was the second largest town. Most places were a mixture of races, who found comfort in living among others but for the most part, they usually stayed close to their birth homes and the Arglar as far as anyone knows, never left the protection of the forest.

The five elders stood in a circle and touched the tips of their wings together. They then flapped them forward once, swirling the dust between them. They touched tips again and stepped to the right twice and then scrapped a right foot across the ground and then flapped forward again, stirring up more dust.

They continued this motion for several minutes. After their tenth cycle they repetitively beat their left wings, which then created a cyclone and then with a quick right wing swept them across the ground and scooped the cyclone up, sending it into the air and then they immediately followed by each biting their tongues and then spit out the blood into the center of their circle.

When the cyclone dropped back to the surface, it picked up the blood and began morphing, shifting into an image. The blood and dust mixed was creating a solid mass which then took the image of a man but not a man but a god. It stood before them, waiting on them to speak.

"As before, you can still address me with your minds. That, I did not take from you." The bloody dust god said.

Elkron stepped forward to speak. "What is it that you shall have us do against this new threat? With one key found and this purple haze that now plagues us, it would appear that your world is in terrible trouble!" He said, looking on at his creator.

"I have spoken with my creator on the urgency that my world needs help, but I am not alone. It seems that other worlds are also having problems with the darkness that has arrived.

"Good news has come from the sole creator and he thinks that he may have a solution to the problem. Since it seems we are threatened with this haze the most he will send help to try to neutralize this world first, but he claims it may take some time.

"This shadow that has cast itself upon our universe has put a halt on our abilities, so I nor any of the other gods have the power to create. Which means I cannot create a hero to save the world as I did before.

"The bad news is that this dark mass has given strength to the creatures of dark and the Nightmare was able to somehow bring forth elemental creatures from his prison to help him retrieve the keys of silence. They are wicked creature's that have the power to annihilate anything. So far, the key hidden in Hazu has been obtained.

"It's only a matter of time before they get the last four keys and free the Nightmare from his prison. My only suggestion to you, is to do your best in protecting the world from this threat until help can arrive.

"Since the powers given to this world still work you should be able to do what you must to try to save it. I'm sorry I can no longer be of any help. Hold out for as long as you can. Help will arrive but when is unknown. Farewell and good luck."

The blood-dust dropped to the ground into a pile. Each elder looked at one another. They all stood motionless in a circle, reflecting on the creator's words. Sagfrin stepped forward and in fluent strokes began scribing in the dirt.

"Who has a plan?"

A Game of Brothers

A desolate world. One of the largest in the universe. Two gods born from darkness. Two brothers stood staring out at an empty rock, void of life.

A large rock floating in an abyss surrounded by stars. One rock of many but this was their world. Their world to do with it as they pleased. The task was simple: "Make it your home. Keep in mind that there are rules that must be followed if you want to remain gods to this planet.

"If you should create a living body, you are the ruler to that which you have created. If you should reveal yourself to a creation of your own design, you forfeit your powers and become mortal yourself. Both of you are linked, so if one should forfeit, the other will be trapped in the spirit realm and be denied any god like properties.

"We gods are a prideful, selfish race and we must uphold our stature as gods. Keep your lives sperate from your creation's lives. There are ways to dabble in their lives, loopholes to make contact if need be. Welcome my children, to your new home."

Rendren and Shalg wandered their world, scoping the layout. They began shifting the dirt and raising mountains. Then they scooped out large holes to contain rivers and large bodies of water. They worked through the mechanics of a water cycle.

Together they pulled nitrogen and oxygen from space and began creating water, then laying it in the designated areas. Once they saw that it all worked without any issues they moved on. They knew that they needed a constant water source to keep the bodies of water plentiful, so they breathed in the water and then lifted it up into the air and then with a powerful wave of their hands, burst the water into molecules and with a mighty breath blew it into the air, creating the atmosphere.

They trapped the oxygen and nitrogen within their world. From there they used their power to begin the creation of everything.

One brother had his own ideas, while the other had his. From there the two brothers had a disagreement about what should inhabit the world. Both had their own agenda about what they wanted to do. That angered them, which sent them on their own paths.

Each brother went to the opposite end of the planet to do their own thing. A divide of sorts.

Once they both were appeased with their work, Rendren challenged his brother to a game of war. His creations versus his creations.

Shalg accepted the challenge. Not for any reason but to the fact that it sounded like fun. Who is the better god? Who is the better creator? A game of strategy!

Since the first time they created and went to war, Shalg had bested Rendren. They would wipe clean the slate and then create again; go to war and repeat. Shalg was victorious every time and that made Rendren envious and caused him to go to desperate measures.

The last game they played, Rendren had created an unstoppable monster which was named the Nightmare, a blood god. Not a legitimate god but a pseudo one upon the planet of Ulderelm.

The Nightmare that Rendren created, was such a threat that Shalg had to actually create a hero who could stop him. The draw back was the hero could only incapacitate the Nightmare and not fully destroy it, so it had to be locked away, in hopes it would never escape.

Since then the game has been on hold, waiting for a player to make his move, for Rendren to make his move but it never came. Years came and went, and he never made his move. Shalg was actually starting to worry about his brother, despite their differences. Rendren had never took this long to make a move.

Shalg wanted to check in on his brother but his own stubborn pride and selfishness got in the way, so Shalg never went. Now the purple haze was here, and it has given power to Rendren's creations over Shalg's, which was a problem.

When Shalg called out to the other gods for answers, his brother was not there. Usually his brother would sense such things as all gods did and meet him at council.

After the council, he returned to his side of Ulderelm and remained, still ever waiting for his brother to make his move and on the council to send help. Now without the power to create, Ulderelm will suffer major catastrophe and he will have to witness it all, until the veil failed.

To Save The Universe or Not

"Cörå... Cörå... Cörå!" A mysterious voice said.

She sat up in a panic. The voice gave her chills that froze her bones. She glanced out the window, wondering what time it was but clearly had forgotten about the haze that dwells upon Buriece now.

She glanced over at Viå who was still asleep. Now a year old and her features had really started to set in even more. She was similar to the Ördük's but since she had her mother's blood flowing through her made her very different.

Viå, being half Cörå and half Tåm gave her a unique overall appearance. She looked about the age of five, when comparing her to the regular children of Åsülrid and Nülån and just as the Ördük's and her father Tåm, she was very smart, way beyond her years. Cörå had not really been around other children to really compare Viå's intelligence to them but she knew she was special.

After she bathed herself and Viå, she went about her daily routines by making sure the kingdom of Nülån was running smoothly in accordance to Buriece. So far there was peace and they hoped it would remain that way.

Though the day went on as it normally did, Cörå could not get the voice out her head. She wondered who and what it was. Mildly distracted for a moment she was pulled away from her thoughts when a knock came from her door.

"Yes, come in!" She said.

The door opened, and it was The Three, Cåg, Jåü and Tåqör. A very unexpected surprise.

"This is a sudden surprise but a good one." She said with a smile.

Even though she did see them on an almost daily basis, the fact that they all showed up at the same time at this time, was a little out of sorts. She didn't quite know what time of day it was, but she knew it had to be early.

"Uhm, Cörå something has arrived upon our world that you must see immediately. We can't really explain it, but it has called for you." Cåg said, adjusting a glove.

"Yeah, a bizarre floating ball of light speaking Cörå's name is really hard to explain." Jåü said sarcastically towards Cåg's comment.

Cörå rose up from her seat and put on her baldric. "Show me!" She ordered.

Upon leaving she went to Viå's room where she was playing with her dolls that her grandfather made for her.

"Hey beautiful." Cörå said as she kneeled down beside her daughter and brushed a finger across her soft cheek.

"Hi, mommy." Viå said, placing a doll in a little chair.

"Viå, we need to leave and go check on something. Would you like to come with us or would you rather stay her with Leesi until I return?" Cörå asked.

Leesi was one of Cörå's closest girlfriends next to Låhüinå. Even though she was Cörå's maiden, she didn't like to treat her as such, so she called her a friend.

"I want to come with you Mommy." Viå answered.

Cörå scooped up Viå and placed her upon her shoulders as she always did. She passed Leesi in the hall and told her that she would be back soon and to pass on the information to anyone that wanted to see her.

All five of them made their way out of castle Nülån and down Cårnik mountain and through Nülån village. The Three lead Cörå out to the training grounds that were once Kråg's but now Cörå had turned it into a nice tribute to the fallen warriors that died in the battle for peace.

Though it was still a place for training,

Cörå had built a wall and had an Ördük by the name of Tåqri carve all the names of those who died into the wall as a memorial.

She also had a florist plant wild flowers around the entire grounds. It was now a beautiful place. Cörå believed that recruits would be more at ease during an extensive day of training with beautiful scenery to look at.

As they exited the training grounds they were on their way towards Åsülrid.

"How much further and why would this... Ball of light not just show up on my doorstep?" She asked more to herself.

"On our way back from Åsülrid, we had just passed the statue of you, when suddenly a light brighter than the sun, as far as I can remember, since before this damn darkness came and polluted our sky. It stopped before us and called your name." Tåqör said scratching his beard that he had grown as a tribute to his brother Tåm.

"Such a random area to show up at!" Cörå said.

Up over a small hill she could see light. It was bright white against the purple haze. Viå being up on Cörå's shoulders had a clear view of the light, as did Tåqör, being so tall.

"Mommy, I see a ball of light!" She said and got a little excited, squirming on her mother's shoulders.

From the top of the hill there was the ball of light, next to her statue that Tåm had carved for her and was placed upon the once divide to remind everyone of her greatness. She thought it was too much and didn't think it was necessary but Jhördån would not hear any such thing from her and believed it was the thing to do. So here it was to sit indefinitely.

As they approached the blinding light, Cörå set Viå down and ordered her to stay with her uncle's. She met up with the floating light mass. It spoke aloud to her.

"Cörå?" The ball of light asked.

"I am Cörå and who are you?" She asked curiously, squinting against the brightness.

"My name is Kyö and I'm from a planet

called Cenuu and I have been ordered from the sole creator to retrieve help from here and take it to another world. I called out to you earlier but got no response, so I searched for others who could assist me.

"I have brought a message and have been instructed to have you hear it." The light dimmed slightly, then back to blinding.

"So, that was the voice I heard in my sleep?" Cörå mentioned aloud to herself.

A voice that was not Kyö's thundered out of the light.

"Cörå this message is urgent, and it requires a great sacrifice on your part. This dark haze that has plagued us and that has affected the entire universe has caused great unbalance. In these dire times and a hero is needed and this is where you come in. Your service is required but not you directly. It is your daughter... Viå."

"What?!" Cörå interrupted. "Stop the message!" She yelled. Cörå looked at her daughter and looked to the ball of light. She had no idea what purpose her daughter had with this haze, but she knew it couldn't be good.

The Three looked at her puzzled and Viå was too occupied with chasing a butterfly to notice her mother's outburst. Her innocence and pure heart was not ready to be foiled with whatever burden the creator had in mind.

Cörå turned back towards Kyö, the strange intelligent ball of light. She didn't want to hear more but she was very curious. "Please continue." She regretted saying.

"The threat that has befallen a planet known as Ulderelm has exceeded greatly with a darkness that only your daughter has the power to potentially neutralize. I believe, that your daughter, has the power to bring balance back to the universe by vanquishing this threat on another planet called Ulderelm.

"If she succeeds, I plan to send her on to the next planet and so forth until the darkness in vanished. I understand your pain, for all of my children are in distress by this new threat and are at risk to parish, including you and your world.

"As of now Viå is the only known partial god in the universe that can hopefully save us. Just know that I would not have sent Kyö to retrieve such a delicate item if I did not trust him. He will take your daughter from here and they together will travel the expanse of the universe. He will teach her many things along the way and know she will not forget you.

"Kyö has the ability to absorb thoughts and memories and if you would like to transfer your whole life and things you would want Viå to know, you can. Kyö will simply go into your mind and soak up whatever you like.

"Know, that time is an issue and they must leave at once, so say your goodbye's and know that she will be taken care of and with hope you may one day be reunited." The message ended.

Cörå dropped to her knees in the grass. Tears of pain and sorrow fell from her eyes. It was a hard choice but then it was not really a choice at all. She could keep Viå here and potentially destroy the universe or let Viå go and potentially save the universe. The only thing was, Viå was barely a child. How can a child save a world and the universe?

Viå came up behind her mother and hugged her, then kissed her cheek. "Don't cry mommy, it's okay." She said, resting her head on Cörå's shoulder.

Cörå pulled her daughter in close and hugged her tightly and never wanted to let her go. Behind her, she heard The Three approach. She didn't know what to do. Could she be selfish?

"My Queen is everything all right?" Tåqör asked as he shielded his eyes with a hand.

"No. Not at all." She said turning to face them as she picked up her daughter and holding her as an infant. "I'm left with a decision that really isn't a decision at all." She said.

Now she knew how Kråg felt, not really having a choice. He could have decided to live through her, as a part of her but in his heart, he knew that true death was the only way. He couldn't bear to give himself; his wickedness to the pureness of Cörå's heart.

She thought about Buriece and the people, and the duty she had sworn to uphold. This decision could save them or destroy them, and it was on her shoulders. She had no idea on how to make this choice. A moment ago, the world was just going about another day and now it went to shit.

Viå would be on her own and traveling with a stranger. Who would comfort her, in her time of need? Who would teach her the ways of womanhood?

She figured she could, since this Kyö is an absorbance. She could explain everything in Viå's life she will face as a woman and also bring her a peace of mind. It wouldn't be enough, but it would be just enough to comfort her whenever she needed it.

She looked at her friends who were stricken with worry. She really could not find the words that would make the situation any better because there was none, they didn't exist.

"So, it would seem that this..." She waved a hand in the air, while fighting back tears. "Purple haze, this darkness has affected the gods throughout the entire universe and has rendered them all powerless.

"The sole creator, the one who has birthed everything into existence has requested help, my help. Not really me actually but has left a heavy burden upon my shoulders. It requires a choice that I must make immediately.

"The creator seems to think, or rather believes that this haze can be neutralized and be brought back into balance but only by the one whom he believes has the power to do it. That one he believes is... Viå." She said, tears welling up again.

"What the shit?" Jåü said, shocked.

"Are you serious?!" Cåg asked, sounding skeptical, adjusting his hat.

They all stood quietly, not really knowing what to say. Jåü turned away and stormed off, cursing. Tåqör didn't say anything. The giant just reached out and embraced Viå. He must have sensed that the decision was clear.

"So, the future of the universe as of now rests upon my decision, my choice. If I don't send her then none of us have a future but if I do send her there's a chance that we might have a future, with the maybe of seeing her again or she fails and we're back at one." Cörå mentioned, placing a hand on her forehead, gripping on the emotions trying to spill out.

Jåü reached out and motioned for Viå. Tåqör handed her over. He hugged her and kissed her cheek. "I love Viå, forever and always." He whispered to her.

"This is ridiculous! This is going to scare the shit out of her!" Cåg said in an outrage.

"I have not fully made my mind up! Last year we lost Tåm and now I'm being asked to lose Viå! How am I supposed to do this? How can anyone be asked to make a choice this heavy? This isn't fair!" Cörå retorted.

"We're talking about our lives and the lives

of thousands upon thousands of other people or whatever that... Thing is!" Jåü said pointing at Kyö.

"Either way you look at the situation, there is no right choice. The universe is ending and if she can save it then it's a risk you might want to consider taking.

"She's part you and she's part Tåm and both of you are strong and smart and you can see that she has your guys' charisma and you know she'll have your valor as well." Tåqör said.

"But she's too young to understand and she'll grow up without those around her, who love her. If she stayed here, then we all can be together until the end. We could live our last days in peace, without worries and when the time comes we can comfort one another." Cörå suggested, knowing full well that would not be true.

"I'm going to have to say that's some shit thinking! I know you and right now you're acting like a scared child hiding from the future.

"When Kråg came and murdered your aunt's, you chased his ass down. You trained with us and then you destroyed him, by yourself without the need of our skills. Then you did something even harder, you popped a baby out of your flower!

"You're not one to give up and her staying here is giving up. Hiding is giving up. The future depends on Viå and you even said you would someday see her again." Jåü said, sounding irritated which was very unlike him and only moments ago he was upset by this.

"There's no guarantee of that. There's no guarantee of anything. What if she doesn't even make it to the destination? How am I going to live without her?! Everyday a part of me will be missing!" Cörå said, broken.

"I think your plan to stay here and die together sounds like the better choice and besides, we don't even know how long we have left. What if the universe dies right after she leaves?" Cåg mentioned.

"The shit you on about? You've always been one to go head first into battle! Now you're being a bitch!" Jåü retorted.

"I am, but this isn't a battle and it's out of our control and she's a little girl! A helpless little girl!" Cåg said, right in Jåü's face.

Cörå heard enough to understand how her beloved friends felt about her burden and together they struggled with the same things she was inside.

She turned and faced the statue, not really looking at it but remembering Tåm. The statue represented how he felt about her, how he had envisioned her, captured her essence. A dedicated and devoted woman and powerful.

His work was the same dedication and devotion and it too was powerful. His work put a person in a state of emotions, feelings and gave peace of mind.

She needed to be this woman now, for the sake of the future. All her friends were right. Viå was just a child and she would be devoted to the task once old enough and she knew that

Viå would have the same valor as well. Though regrettably, she made her decision, as painful as it was but right was right.

She turned back to her friends. "I have made my decision!"

Cåg and Jåü stopped arguing and looked at her. She approached Cåg and placed a comforting hand on his cheek.

"My friend. My protector. The greatest swordsmen in all of Buriece. Be at ease that I will suffer greater than you. This choice has begun breaking my heart already and not one day shall go by that I won't regret my decision.

"We must have faith in her that she can restore the universe. We must hope to save this world and every other by this choice." She said with heavy tears.

She looked at all of them, fighting back the tears. "We can all leave a memory and some guidance of ourselves for Viå with Kyö, who can show them to her whenever she is in need. I will go first." She said and walked over to Kyö.

All three sat down with Viå who was pulling up grass and making a pile. Not one of them said a word. Viå got up and ran over to Cåg and took his hat off and then ran back to her grass pile and started to fill up the hat.

"You're a silly child aren't you Viå?" Cåg questioned.

She ignored him and finished filling the hat up. Once it was full, she dumped it on her own head. Everyone laughed, even her. She approached Tåqör and put the hat upon his massive head. His head made the hat look as if it was made for a doll.

Jåü laughed extremely hard at the sight. Viå kissed Tåqör on his nose then removed the hat and placed it upon Jåü's greasy head.

"Very fitting, do you think?" Jåü asked Viå. She nodded, with a big grin.

Jåü jumped up and started acting like Cåg. His movements were a complete over exaggeration. "I'm the greatest swordsmen that ever lived and the most handsome of all the men except my best friend Jåü. He is much better looking than I and gets all the girls!" He mimicked looking at Viå, making her giggle.

"Uncle Jåü, you're funny!" Viå said, laughing. Cåg just rolled his eyes. Tåqör seemed to be enjoying it.

Cörå had finished with her messages to Viå and showed up just in time as Jåü tossed the hat back on Cåg's head, perfectly. Cåg picked it up and smoothed his hair back and then again placed his hat upon his head.

"Who's next?" She asked.

"I'll go." Tåqör said. The giant picked himself up off the ground and walked off towards Kyö.

"Viå, I need to have a talk with you." Cörå said.

"Okay, mommy." Viå said and jumped in her mother's arms. They embraced, Cörå kissed her on the lips. They walked off a way, for a little privacy. They both sat down in the grass.

"You see that ball of light over there?" Cörå said, pointing. Viå nodded. "His name is Kyö and he's really nice." She continued but questioned her words, since she didn't know him at all but if the creator trust's him then she should too, she figured.

"You are going to go with him, on a trip." She said and tried her damnedest not to cry. "I can't go with you; so, you will be alone with Kyö. He is sworn to take good care of you." She added, as tears rolled down.

Viå showed no emotions to her words. She wasn't sure if Viå fully understood what she was saying. Viå, just looked down at the grass.

"You are a very important girl and you are needed for an important task. You are called upon to be a hero." Cörå said, running a hand through Viå's hair.

"Like you and my uncle's and my daddy was?!" Viå asked.

"Exactly! Just like us. I want you to know that I'll be with you, right here." She said and touched Viå on her head. "In your brain. Whenever you want, you just think of me." She concluded.

"And daddy and Cåg and Jåü and Tåqör and Grandpa Tråqöy!" Viå added.

"Them too, of course. Also, Kyö can show you me and your uncle's whenever you like and your daddy. You just say; "show me my mommy and daddy please and he will show you. Do you understand?" She asked, lifting her daughter's face up to look into her eyes.

Viå nodded that she understood. All of this was too much and too sudden. In a few moments Viå would be gone without any knowledge of when she might return. The thought was haunting.

Cörå couldn't think of anything else to say. The departure was going to be very overwhelming and frightening for her. It would be worse for Viå; her not fully comprehending the situation. Cörå was sure that once it was time, Viå would lose her shit.

The Three had finished with Kyö and were standing, waiting for Cörå to finish with Viå. Cörå picked her up and they both headed towards, the three of them.

"Let us not make this to heart breaking because that could cause Viå to panic and freak out. So, let us stay as strong as possible and wait on our emotions until they have left." Cörå said, choking back the urge to sob.

Everyone nodded, then the five headed to Kyö, who was still floating and glowing and waiting patiently. They stood before him. Cörå didn't want to put Viå down.

"Viå, this is Kyö." Cörå introduced.

"How nice to finally meet you. I'm glad we will be traveling together. You are going to have so much fun seeing things that few others have seen. Besides the gods, of course." Kyö said.

Viå, asked to be put down. She walked over to Kyö and reached out her hand to touch him. "He's so soft and warm!" Viå said and giggled. She rubbed her hands all over his orb form.

Viå turned and ran to Cörå. They embraced again a Cörå gave her a long kiss. "I love you baby and I'll see you again when you return." She said.

Tåqör, reached down and picked her up and pulled Viå in for a hug and then kissed her nose. "I love you little one. Think of me often." He said and set her back down.

Jåü knelt down and hugged her tightly in his arms. He held her for a moment and breathed in her hair, taking in the scent. "Viå, you're strong like your momma and your dad. You are a very special person and I'm so glad you're in my life. I'll be waiting on your return. I love you." He said.

"Viå, I want you to have this." Cåg said as he laid his baldric and swords down at her feet. "I gave your father my old swords by the sea as a tribute and now I'm giving you my new ones. I want you to practice with them every day when you're strong enough to wield them of course." He mentioned and pushed her hair back behind her ears.

Cörå held Viå's hand and picked up Cåg's gift as they turned back towards Kyö. As they got closer, Kyö's side opened, revealing a place to sit inside. Viå stopped. She looked up at her mom.

"Mommy, I'm scared!" She said nervously. Cörå picked her up and hugged her tightly for the last time.

"Honey, there's nothing to be afraid of. You will be safe. Kyö will protect you. Just remember that you can see me anytime you ask him. I will see you... soon. I love you baby." Cörå said and set Viå down inside Kyö and placed Cåg's baldric, sword, and scabbard down at her feet, next to a bag that was full of things to consume.

Viå started to cry and tried to climb out of Kyö. Cörå held her to the seat and hushed her. "Baby, you're going to be okay. Remember you're going to be a hero like me and daddy! It's time for you to be strong. Calm down my big, strong, girl. We're with you always." Cörå softly mentioned trying to sound confident, trying keep her composer.

Viå sat quietly, crying. Tears rolled down her cheeks, clearly upset. She looked out at her uncles who were waving at her. She crossed her arms over her chest and looked down. "I love you mommy!"

"I love you too!" Cörå responded.

Kyö closed himself. "It was nice to meet you all and I promise, I will take good care of her." He said and closed himself up and then rose up into the air. He climbed higher and higher until his light was no longer visible in the haze.

Cörå dropped to the ground with a broken heart. She let out a horrifying scream of pain. The Three all knelt around her and hugged her. She continued to shrill out in shrieks of pain. There was nothing anyone could say or do to comfort a mother losing a child. They knew she would be back one day but there was no comfort in that.

Better Late Than Never

Ulderelm was unrecognizable. A world that was once peaceful and full of life was now in chaotic shambles. Any pure inhabitants prior to the escape of the nightmare was murdered or placed into slavery.

Only one village was left standing in all of Ulderelm and that was Drenchin. The rest were burned down. Most Molgren's and enslaved creatures and a few humans, lived in Drenchin.

To keep food and supplies in demand. Slaves were put to work, mostly where items of importance were most beneficial to keep them alive.

The slaves slept outside; rain or not. It's

been years since any one of them had a bath. They were offered two meals a day, which consisted of whatever the Molgren's threw at them, which wasn't much.

The five elders did everything they could against the threat, but their powers were useless. They had failed at every attempt to succeed. Each elder fled during the pivotal moment they realized they could not save their people. Cowards as they were; they felt their duty solely rested on the hero who was supposed to arrive in the near future. They knew they had to survive to help this savior. To help them succeed.

The last however many years the Nightmare has been tearing the world apart in search of the elders and all but two have been captured. Together, the elder's blood contained more power than anything on Ulderelm and he would not stop, until the last two were found. His elemental pixes still scurry the land in search of the two elusive elders. How the two elders eluded them for so long was a mystery, but the Nightmare knew they would find them.

"It's been years and the gods have not made true their promise of a savior!" Sagfrin etched in frustration.

"We must have faith!" Elkron scribbled.

Sagfrin brushed a wing across the ground, pissed by his shit faith. Her world, their world was gone. It would take years to set it right. The beings that remained, could most likely not hold a tool from being so malnourished and could no longer fight even if they wanted to.

Most wished for death every day. Some tried but the dark one's stopped them. The Nightmare had a whole mass of creatures and beasts and they were ordered to not hurt any slaves and to keep them alive so that they can fulfill their daily tasks of keeping the desolate world in some kind of order.

Any who did step out of line or tried to take their life were heavily monitored to ensure they remained physically capable of maintaining their daily contribution. The elders witnessed this first hand and had almost been captured. They were lucky to have escaped that time.

Now they were so far off the map that they wondered if they would even know if the savior had arrived. The hero could already be in Ulderelm searching for them, or someone to lead them to their destination.

"How are we supposed to know when this potential hero will arrive?!" Sagfrin scratched.

"I trust that we will get a sign of some kind." Elkron added.

Sagfrin needed to get some air. They have been hiding in a cave for years. Only heading out when they were at their peak of starvation. She had had enough. She turned her back on Elkron and ascended the tunnel of mazes. He tried to stop her, but she shrugged him off. He raced in front of her and stopped, blocking her way. She scowled at him. She waved a wing and tossed him to the side. Not hard but her enough to make a point.

She had been listening to him for years, following on blind faith, on hope. She was finished with the gods, with the savior. She was done with Elkron.

Sagfrin turned right, then left, following the maze towards the entrance. Another left, then another right. The maze could have confounded an intruder for days, but they have been in it for years, so it was a simple pattern.

The air began to get cooler and filled her lungs. She was almost there. She knew Elkron was trailing her because he would not leave her alone by herself, but she was no longer going to take to hiding. If her fate was getting caught, then she accepted it, because this has gone on for far too long and it was time to do something; not hide.

In the last few years or so they both had watched the world around them transform into a wasteland filled with Molgren's, who populated Ulderelm like mad and they were all under the Nightmare.

It didn't start that way. First the beasts were

free and began terrorizing towns. Murdering, raping, and looting. Then the final key of silence was found and that was what had changed everything.

Elkron and Sagfrin were there to bear witness to the Nightmare's freedom. The four elemental sprites were there, welcoming their leader. They were the reason for the keys of silence, being taken.

The last key needed all four of them combined to obtain it. Somehow the Nightmare knew that the five elders had used the elements to seal away the keys. How the Nightmare was able to summon the creatures had also eluded them.

Moudrous was a deep hollowed mine, once used for its abundance of precise alloy called Greenite, which was used to create armor and weapons. It was the strongest metal on Ulderelm.

When the plan to imprison the Nightmare was set in motion. They needed a place to put him, to seal him away indefinitely. So, the elders banished the workers and ordered them to never return. They set up wards using the metal within. The alloy worked well as a source to hold the power indefinitely.

It was a powerful light source, taken from the sun, to keep the Nightmare weak, trapped. Since he could not be destroyed, their only chance of succeeding was keeping him frail and locked away.

When the five keys were placed into the Gate of Moudrous by the elemental sprites, it burst into fragments and littered the ground. Thick dust billowed out of the mine from years of lying dormant. Out of the thick dark grey cloud came a scream of death. Blood red eyes glowed bright. Two massive black wings stretched wide. The white sharp fangs, stood out against the opaque smog.

In one massive black hand with long, thick, maroon nails, equally as formidable as it's fangs, held the Scepter of Tribulation. The Nightmare, in his need to gloat had told

Thondrous that it was once a god who had devoted its life to causing catastrophic terror of an astronomical scale. Who, when pursued by the one creator and his fellowship of gods, went into hiding and had then altered itself into the scepter to forever live on to continue causing chaos.

With the flare of his wide nostrils the Nightmare looked towards his elemental sprites. "I smell fear. Fear from those who oppose me. Go forth and find the five elders and bring them to me; alive." He said and lifted his free hand, palm up, an image appeared of Elkron. "This is an image of what they look like. Now go." He ordered. The sprites immediately took off.

The Nightmare was a frightening figure. He stood naked and brooding, with skin as black as a moonless night.

He scowled with his thick black brows. His jaw was tightly compressed, making the muscles in his face bulge. He was thick skinned with a heavy muscular build.

He was twice as large as any mere man and creature. Though his traits were similar to that of a human, as far as anatomy and structure go but he was not a man but a creature of darkness. A beast that could not be killed and now, a monster that had no one to stand against him. He was free to do what he wished.

The Nightmare turned and waved the scepter across the opening of the mine. The earth began to shake and then the mine caved in. A large crater was all that was left of the Nightmare's prison.

One mighty jump and a thrust of his wings and the nightmare was in the air. He took off, North. Sagfrin and Elkron ducked beneath a bush. They knew they had to warn the other elders.

Sagfrin stood at the mouth of the cave looking out over Valley mountain, called that because of the many valleys it had. They were far from civilization, what was left of it anyways. Elkron came and stood next to her.

She had tears in her eyes. She felt like everything she represented was gone. Her purpose erased. Her home was taken and is now the lair of what can't be destroyed.

Was Ulderelm forsaken by the sole creator? Did he just forget about them? Their creator said it would be soon and it's been years.

Her and Elkron have been running and hiding, ever since. She was exhausted. She just wanted to be back in her home; back in her bed. She wanted to take a long soothing bath.

Her only contact the entire time had been Elkron and she was thankful that he stayed head strong and by her side the whole time. Although the mental anguish that weighed on them was ever present. The normality's of life still came.

When they needed to forage, they did but since the destruction of Ulderelm, resources were hard to come by. They had to recently sneak into one of the slave compounds and risk being captured in order to get their fill.

Other needs arose as well such as the need to mate. Mostly it was a way to escape from the reality of what was happening. She was first to offer herself up to Elkron. She wondered if he ever got aroused and if so, he never made himself vulnerable to the cravings.

It was just before they were getting ready to sleep. The air was cool, and they were both bundled together to stay warm. She turned into him with her head, rubbing it on his chest. He felt good, cozy and comforting. She pressed into him, nuzzling the feathers on his chest. He in turn did the same on her head. He wrapped her in his wings and held her tightly. The two came together. It felt wrong during such a time, but it also felt right.

That was first of many in what felt like a years' time. She didn't know if she loved him on an intimate level, but she did have respect for him, that was for sure and as a friend she did love him.

She was curious, that if it was under normal circumstances, if things could have ended up the way they were between them now. Most likely, but not since they have not seen each other in thousands of years and they only reconnected because of the darkness. She did have to admit, she was enjoying his presence and his strong sexual appetite.

She looked over at him and he turned to her. He wrapped a wing over her shoulders and hugged her. Though she was an elder and full of power, she still at times needed to be comforted. They both stood, looking out at the mountains. Free from threat and void of life. They felt alone in the world.

Out in the distance in the purple haze. A shooting star flew across the sky, lighting it up as it soared through. It's been years since they've seen a shooting star, let alone actual stars and now here one was. Unlike a normal shooting star, this one kept traveling until it touched down into the distance.

Elkron and Sagfrin gave each other a look. Then excitement filled them. Sagfrin's feathers ruffled and she took off in a rush and Elkron was not far behind. The two soared through the air, beating their wings. A strong head wind was making their progression a bit challenging.

The distance of the fallen star had to be at least five to seven miles. Elkron was hoping that this was their answer to saving Ulderelm. The problem was; who else had witnessed the shooting star. They needed to get to it first before any other eyes that had watched its descent did.

They have only gone roughly a mile, and both were getting exhausted. Sagfrin, so desperate for a savior was not going to give up. She continued to thrust herself into the wind. It was like an invisible force was preventing them from getting to their intended target.

Instantly a gust of wind, so powerful thrust them backwards, somersaulting them through the air. They both flapped wildly, trying to counteract the sudden blast of force. Once in control, down in a ravine they spotted the elemental sprites that had freed the Nightmare and were searching for them.

The wind sprite was the reason for their sudden tumble. The other three were no threat to them at this time but that can change if they don't think through this problem. Fear had now set in and they were both tired from fighting against the head wind caused by the wind elemental sprite. They landed a good distance away from the sprites, for they had no idea what kind of threat they faced. They needed a plan and now. The fallen star was threatened by every passing minute.

Elkron quickly motioned his wings outward and around, suggesting they both fly wide around the wind sprite. Sagfrin nodded her consensus. The only problem with this plan was the wind sprite could go after one of them and potentially capture them, but they needed to do something.

A loud crash erupted and echoed from behind them. Out in the distance the wind sprite was taking up rocks and hurling them at them. Then suddenly it picked up the other three elemental sprites and launched them in their direction. The time to follow through with their plan was now.

They pushed off in opposite directions and didn't look back. From the sound, Elkron knew he was being pursued. Wise plan from creatures that seemed so animalistic. He figured that they sensed that he was the leader and by capturing him the other would give up, which wasn't far from the truth.

Filled with worry, not for his own safety but for Sagfrin, he looked to his left to try and catch a glimpse of her. She was racing through the air without any threat at all. The sound of wind was gaining on him. He quickened up his pace but before he knew it, he was flipping around. The world spun around him.

The ground was coming up fast. He hit hard and rolled through the dirt. Pain shot through him. He needed to get up and quickly. He tried but a sharp pain rushed through his body. His left wing was broken. He could feel it swelling up. He swung his good wing around in a circle collecting the air and formed a shield around himself.

He took off on foot, looking towards the sky. There was no sign of Sagfrin. He would hope she would have enough sense to get to that fallen star in search of answers. Being as he was, running was not his area of physical qualities. His kind was made for flight, not running. They were not like most creatures of Ulderelm.

A dust cloud engulfed him. He knew this was not good. This sprite was going to be the end of him. Hopefully his shield would keep him safe. The dust around him started to turn into mud, wrapping around his shield. He was now cocooned, trapped within a shell of mud and then it began to get warm, really warm within the confines of his security shield. They were encasing him in a prison of hard clay.

Without the use of his other wing, his powers were limited, and he knew that he could not blast the hardened mud off. Suddenly he started to move. He could feel himself rising in the air. Possibly being transported by the wind sprite. He really expected Sagfrin to do her duty because his time has come.

Sagfrin, in an emotion of panic did not stop. She never once looked back. She knew Elkron could handle himself and she was quite sure he would be meeting up with her. The chances of one of them being captured was a reality and if that were to happen they would still have to fulfill their duty to Ulderelm.

Another mountain and she should be at the point of the fallen star. She was beat and needed a long rest but that was not an option. If that star was indeed the savior, she needed to get to it and then get him or her to safety. Waiting for Elkron was also out of the question. He would find them, she was positive.

At the peak of the next mountain top, a

bright glow radiated from beyond. Sagfrin had not seen such a beautiful sight in a long time. The dark purple murky cloud has been the setting for years. This light was a god send.

Hope filled her and gave her a boost of energy. Tears formed in her eyes as she rushed to get to the source of the light. Was she being to rash, to hopeful? Was she getting ahead of herself? This could, all together not be the savior but another nightmare.

Over the peak, down in a forest, she could see the light. It was bright as the sun. She had to squint to see her landing and then she got behind a large bush to watch. The light did not move. She suddenly heard a voice, followed by another. It was a male and a female voice. They were distinguished enough to tell what gender but not loud enough to hear what was being spoken.

She slowly made her way down the embankment, being careful not to slip on the thick grass. Inching her way down, she stopped and stood motionless, listening. The voices were now whispers. She held her breath and closed her eyes and opened her ears to focus just on their voices alone. They were still too quiet.

The bright glow of light instantly went dim but not enough to disappear. She made her way closer to the whispers. When she was finally in ear shot, she stopped and leaned into a tree.

"Was there any more information about what I was supposed to do once I arrived here?" The female voice asked.

"No. Only the same thing I've filled you in on over the last few days. You're supposed to..." The males voice was interrupted by the females.

"Save Ulderelm and try to dissipate the constant darkness; yeah, yeah, I know!" She said, sounding annoyed.

"We should try to find someone who knows something. Anyone who may have answers." The male voice suggested.

"Hey! You! The one lurking in the trees!"

The female voice said. The voice didn't come from the direction the two were located, it was in her head. She went evermore still. Trying to blend in with the tree.

"Come out. I'm not going to hurt you. We're not going to hurt you. I knew you were here since you came over the top of that mountain. Good job on not making noise. If I didn't have my perfect hearing, I may have never known." The female voice said, clearly trying to ease any fear.

Sagfrin was at a loss; she was caught but she still had a chance to flee and this was confirmed the savior. She was the wisest of the five elders and though not quite as strong as her male alliance, she fancied herself as a powerful Cremhen, she often thought more so than the others.

The problem was, with Ulderelm in its darkest days, she was doubting her own strengths and rightfully so, being she put everything on Elkron, which made her grow soft and dependable upon him. She was going to have to apologize to him when he arrived. If he arrived.

Lost in her own thoughts, she did not notice, nor did she hear anyone coming but there beside her was the most beautiful woman, she had ever seen. She has seen some attractive humans in Ulderelm but this one would cause any mortal man his own death.

She was tall, slim, and very muscular. The little weight around her face, which was for the most part, non-existent, revealed her to be fairly young, almost still a child. Her beautiful long blonde hair was almost golden against her dark skin. Her skin wasn't black, more of a grey in color. Her eyes were a gorgeous hazel and slightly larger than a typical human. She had a delicate nose that was almost too cute, which made her lips look voluptuous.

She had a very kind face but Sagfrin could tell that this creature was a very deadly force. She had on a black baldric that carried two swords with white handles on her back. She wondered how sharp her skills were with them.

The clothes she wore were very tight fitting that left almost nothing to the imagination. It was definitely not of this world. It was a blue single piece from the ankle up to her shoulders and tapered to a V at her chest, which exposed quite a lot of her breasts. It had no sleeves, which was very unlike this world. On her feet were a thick dark brown boot of some kind.

Sagfrin had never seen anything like her or her attire before. Sagfrin had a lot of questions that had to wait because those elemental sprites could at any moment start attacking. Plus, she needed to intervene with Elkron, if he made it.

"We cannot linger, for there are things that are in pursuit of me and my companion, so we need to be off, now!" Sagfrin scratched in a bare patch in the grass, urgently, then turned and started walking away.

"Uhm. Excuse me but we're trying to locate answers, so that we can save this world and the threat of the universe!" The woman said.

"Then, you have found the right one with

answers, but we can't do it here!" Sagfrin returned to the bare spot, swiped, then scribbled and continued on.

"Honestly, you can communicate with me by projecting your thoughts, so you don't have to keep writing!" The blonde hair beauty said to Sagfrin's mind.

"I suggest you get your friend and follow!" Sagfrin stated mentally.

"Kyö, let's go!" The woman loudly whispered. "My friend can fly so we can follow!" She added, directing her thoughts towards Sagfrin.

Sagfrin stopped when she heard the crashing of trees being snapped and falling down. Fear over took her when she laid eyes on the woman's friend. It was a large round glowing thing, which was quite large and if it was sitting on the ground the woman and the orb would be the same height.

An area opened on the side of her friend, revealing a place to sit. The woman pulled free her swords and placed them beneath the seating area and then she jumped inside. The woman looked kind of ridiculous seated within, since she was so tall. So many questions.

"Lead the way and we will follow. By the way my name is Viå and this is Kyö." Viå said.

"How very nice to meet you." Kyö said.

"I am Sagfrin, one of five elders, the peace keepers of Ulderelm and it's nice to meet, now we must be off!" Sagfrin said and ascended into the air.

"That was rude, she didn't say anything!" Kyö said to Viå as he followed the strange winged creature.

"She did, to me. Her name is Sagfrin and she seems to be the one we were looking for." Viå said.

Manacled

"**W**here is the last elder?!" The Nightmare asked in his deep scratchy voice.

Elkron said nothing, obviously he couldn't if he wanted too. He stood in what used to be Sagfrin's main chamber. His wing burned and throbbed. It was never going to heal properly without the proper care and he knew that would never come. He eyed the Nightmare up and down. He truly was an ugly, freak of a beast but Elkron had too much faith in his allies and the future of Ulderelm to give up any information. He would die, taking it to his early demise.

The Nightmare had no guards, he clearly believed he did not need any, since he had the scepter and obviously he couldn't be killed. The main chamber was full of fully naked human woman. They all stood to the sides of the room. Four of them were beside his throne, rubbing upon his chest and shoulders.

"Fetch me the Shadow!" He ordered to one of the naked women. She quickly left the room. The Nightmare never took his blood red eyes off Elkron.

"I have your fellowship; here in the cells, where you'll be joining them soon. They too were like you, speechless. They are alive, for now.

"Soon enough I'll have your friend and then I'm going to take each one of you by your puny fucking necks and snap them like twigs and then I'm going to suck the warm, sweet, salty blood from your bodies; every last drop, taking your powers." He stated.

The Nightmare reached over with a hand and grabbed a woman by her dark hair and pulled her into his lap. Not one sound came from her as she dangled by her hair. In his lap she looked like a child. He wrenched her head back, exposing her neck. His long thin maroon tongue licked upon it leaving a trail of thick spit. His massive penis had a mind of its own as it came to life, finding its way to woman's vagina.

Elkron turned his attention away. This was completely disturbing. The woman began moaning, then she let out a short scream of pain. Elkron turned back briefly and the Nightmare was sucking the blood from the woman he was penetrating. Blood was dripping down the woman's back. The nightmare kept pulling on the woman's hair and sucking until her head ripped nearly off her shoulders.

He continued to suck until she was bloodless and didn't stop thrusting until he had finished and then he shoved her lifeless body onto the floor. She landed with a thud before Elkron. His eyes were wide with fear, over the gruesome sight. The nightmare used his long tongue to clean the blood from his face.

Just then the door came open and a cold presence filled the room. Elkron could only hear the steps of the bare foot woman approaching. Chills ruffled his feathers. He could feel the eerie world of death as a voice came from behind him. It was a heavy breathy whisper, which seemed to echo itself.

"My master, you summoned?" The voice asked.

"A group of Molgren's in the Southeast has seen a bright light fall to the surface. You will lead the same group of Molgren's to that location and see if you can find any information on what it was.

"If you find anything, bring it to me and if you happen to find one of these winged fucks, make sure it comes back with you, alive." The Nightmare demanded pointing at Elkron.

"As you desire master." The multiple, whispering voice said. The cold lurking feeling of dread left Elkron as the shadow left the room.

Two large ugly Molgren's came in and grabbed Elkron by the wings and they were not gentle. The pain from his broken wing almost made him pass out. They lifted him off his feet and carried him out of the room. The Nightmare grabbed another woman with red head and made her straddle him. The penis started coming to life again, then the door closed.

Torches with Ever-flame lit the halls as the Molgren's took him down hall after hall. Every stair they came to, they went up. Elkron figured he was being taken to the tower, which made no sense, since the cells were typically in the lower parts of most citadel's.

Now that word has landed upon the Nightmare's ears about the falling star, he sure hoped that it was the help they have been waiting for and that Sagfrin made it to the location safely and if so; hoped too, that she found sanctuary for them, if indeed it was savior that has arrived.

Elkron had to have faith, he had to believe,

that falling star was something special. It was, in their time spent hiding, the only sign of any kind in years. So, he had to believe it was the savior and soon, help would arrive.

They neared a two-door room. The doors were red with a gold trim. They were not heavy, thick doors, so breaking through them was not a problem.

The Molgren's dropped him to the floor. One fondled at a ring full of keys. He slowly grabbed one at a time, inspecting each one thoroughly, before sliding it down and grabbing the next.

These beasts were as dimwitted as one could get. The Molgren looked at each key for approximately one minute a piece. Elkron wondered if he could make it out of the confines of the citadel without these dimwitted beasts ever knowing, but his broken wing was a hindrance and would be the reason he would get caught if he did try to run, since he could not use his powers as easily.

That too was probably why the Nightmare

cared not to bind him and the fact that the Nightmare could not be killed was most likely the main reason as well.

Could he summon an air wisp, knocking them both against the door with one mobile wing? Should he try to free the others, if they are indeed behind the doors? He quickly eyed the hall. Since his wing was busted, flying was not an option, so he didn't bother with looking for an open window or a room to hide and escape from but if he could get the others free, they could escape; easily.

He could see no exit, but he figured he would try to free his fellowship either way and worry about an escape exit after. He'll wait until the dumb Molgren inserted the right key and then he would make his move.

The second Molgren stood watching the first. Both were heavy mouth breathers and the stench that came from them was so foul he wondered how he was still alive.

After another five or so minutes the Molgren found the right key and the funny thing was, it was the only key on the ring that was different from all the others. Unlike the rest, which were the typical loop head with a long shaft, which had two to four teeth cut in various patterns to fit specific locks. This one had a square head with a shorter shaft and small teeth that ran up most of the shaft, not to mention it was gold.

The Molgren inserted the key into the lock and turned it. It clicked, which made the Molgren's chuckle. What little things amused such ugly beasts. They were as children. The doors opened inward into a dark room with torches that burned with an Ever-flame.

The two beasts turned around to reach for him but Elkron gathered up his powers and with maximum effort he swung his good wing forward. The gust of the wind wisp was not as strong as he had hoped but it proved to be somewhat effective.

The Molgren's flew backwards into the room, landing on their backs, sliding across the floor. Now, it was a life and death battle.

Elkron leaped into the air landing on the bigger of the two ugly beasts. He thrust his head downward with his mouth opened wide and clamped down hard and then twisted his head tearing the Molgren's throat out.

Blood shot out as the Molgren reached for his own throat, but he was dead before his hands ever arrived. A stiff kick to Elkron's side, sent him flying across the room hitting the wall with chains. The chains rattled as he hit the floor. The smaller Molgren reached for his broad dagger but did not pull it, just kept it there.

Peculiar as it was, it did make sense. He and the other elders were important to the Nightmare, well their blood was, anyways. He glanced around the room and there they were, still in one piece, shackled and hanging from chains. Elkron pulled again for his power and this time he used the Ever-flame.

He absorbed the heat, taking in the flame within his unbroken wing. He pulled oxygen from the air and made the flame brighter and denser and then he let it fly. It hit and then burst on the Molgren's arms as he tried to block it. It was a failed attempt from the moment Elkron had the flame within his control.

The damn Molgren shook his arms trying to extinguish the Ever-flame but it was a losing battle. He went up in flames and would continue to burn, forever.

Now to free the elders. He picked up the keys and walked to the nearest elder, Jupin who was looking grumpy as ever. Elkron inspected the manacles for a place to insert a key but there was none. Puzzled, he looked at the other one and just as the first, there was nothing.

Elkron has dealt with things of strange powers before and those things took time and right at this moment there was none. Since the elders powers were simply a control over the elements, he just needed to figure out which elements were used to fashion these particular cuffs. They looked like an ordinary solidified mineral mixture of chromium and iron.

He tried to weld it to his powers but achieved nothing. He stood in thought, ignoring the searing pain coursing through his body from the busted appendage. He wished at that moment that they could speak because then they could collaborate on what the shackles were composited from with his fellowship.

He turned at looked at the other two, just hanging there, almost lifeless. Framen and Piko, seemed to have given up. He hasn't given up yet and he was not going to. He refocused on the manacles, thinking about the different types of metal used. He walked over to the ones that he had been kicked into, dangling on the wall. They too were closed with no seams. How were these placed onto a captive? He thought.

No sooner was that questioned answered when he reached out and touched a dangling cuff, instantly he was caught. Now what? Shit! He thought. Now more than ever he needed to figure out the properties of this damn shackle.

He could hear something coming up the corridor. There was no noise, just a feeling. It was there; something was coming.

His mind raced. Frantically he started to pull at the elemental components of the cuff that trapped him. Nothing was working. The feeling from the presence in the hall grew stronger. It was no use, he was fucked.

Elkron looked towards the door and standing within the doorway was a figure in a dark grey woven cloak, which was pulled up over its head. At the hip was a blade that was bright white with a handle that was shaped like a Choroac, which was an animal that was said to be so elusive and impossible to hunt down. Stories said that they were spirits and to catch one would bring you great luck and wealth.

The sandals that the figure was wearing were very different from what this world wore. They had a thick black sole with straps that wound up around the figures muscular calves.

From the feet and partial legs, Elkron assumed it was human.

The figure stepped inside the room and threw the hood of the dark grey woven cloak back. Elkron was aghast at what he saw.

Across the Universe

Sagfrin lead them far, far from Drenchin. As far as they were already, she felt better knowing they were almost twice the distance. She knew not, whether Elkron would be joining them or if he was captured. She sent out good thoughts towards Elkron for a safe journey and that they may find each other, soon.

They all sat on the Southern bank of a massive lake called Lantro, looking out over the purple reflection on the water. The northern part of the lake was an encampment, where the brick makers were located, which had many Molgren's but Sagfrin didn't believe that they posed a threat in their current location.

"So please share what we need to know." Viå asked Sagfrin.

"To sum it up, for time is a thing we no longer have. As you see this world now, it once was long ago a somewhat peaceful land, with villages, farms, and an abundance of life. Now since the Nightmare has been free, it's this." She said, waving a wing around. "The Nightmare has gathered all the creatures of the night, called Molgren's, who are very fast and eat flesh. They are not a wise creature, but deadly and now they no longer hide due to the purple haze that plagues the universe. They are his army, which now inhabit all of Ulderelm, due to their excessive breeding. So, the battle we face will be a hard and deadly one.

"What you truly need to know is there are four elemental sprites roaming the lands, in search of me and my companion, Elkron. We ran into them and got separated. I hope he is okay." She said sounding extremely worried. "Another thing. The Nightmare cannot be killed, and he carries with him the scepter of tribulation, which causes great chaos. It literally can take down mountains with a single wave." Sagfrin added.

Viå sat quietly. She had so many questions. Though she was no longer a child, she was still young and since she spent most of her life traveling within Kyö, she was ignorant to certain things and the only information she gained over the years was from the play-back from her mother and her uncles. Kyö also did his best to answer any questions she had.

"Forgive me, for I am new to certain information. I spent most of my life traveling through the universe. I was just over a year old when I was sent on this quest, so I may ask you some monotonous questions from time to time." Viå said.

Sagfrin looked at her for a moment, letting her mind comprehend that this woman was taken from her family so young to save this world. Sagfrin couldn't help feeling sorry for her. "Ignorant questions are only the ones not asked." Sagfrin said.

"Well then. First what is an elemental sprite?" Viå asked.

"It's a creature that is made up of an element. There are four of them, fire, wind, water, and earth. Each one has the power to control the same elements that they are made of and they can even combine themselves to use the others for an overall advantage.

"Somehow the Nightmare created them from his prison. We are not sure how he did such a thing." Sagfrin added.

Viå was not too sure what an element was but she got the idea, since she knew what fire, water, wind, and earth were. She wondered what a scepter was. "So, what is this scepter of tribulation?" She asked.

"It's like a stick but not. I've never held it nor touched it but from its appearance, I'd say it's made of some type of metal. It's rumored to be a god once, who had turned itself into the scepter. It's a very dangerous weapon of destruction.

"When a created being named Thondrous, that the god of this world created to fight the Nightmare. He succeeded in winning the battle but could not kill him. So, we needed to find a place to lock him away. We, the elders used our powers to place powerful light from the sun into a precious metal called Greenite that used to be mined from where we decided to lock the Nightmare up. We used the Greenite to trap the sun's light to keep the Nightmare weak. When the Nightmare was finished, the scepter was nowhere to be found. He somehow had hidden it with himself when we trapped him in his prison.

"I'm guessing that his strength powers the scepter, which is why he couldn't use it to free himself." Sagfrin said, her expression, baffled.

"So, there's a wicked man, called the Nightmare who wields a scepter god that causes great destruction. Great!" Viå said, concerned.

"He's not a man, he's a beast and he's darker than the deepest cave, who is twice your size and can fly. He's a, well... Nightmare!" Sagfrin stated.

"Shit! Viå said aloud. "Well, I did not come all this way to cower. I've been training with these swords on our many stops along the way since I could hold them. I've been in situations where I've had to use them to get Kyö and I out of some life or death predicaments."

That was not a more truer statement. When her and Kyö would need a rest or she was hungry or simply needed to get out and stretch, they would stop at the nearest planet. Most of them were places, you wished you never set foot in and they never stopped longer than needed but sometimes their departure was delayed due to the things of that world trying to eat them or capture them and simply to just kill them.

This one world they stopped in when Viå was still just a girl, although the darkness consumed it, it was still a beautiful place full of vivid colors and the strangest animals she had ever seen. They stopped there because she was tired of traveling and she really wanted to get in some training; now that she was strong enough to hold the swords in each hand.

They had come into a place where three water falls of blue, green, and yellow water fell into the pool below, where they did not blend together but stayed separate. In the sky beyond were five rainbows, sitting out in the distance, just barely visible in the haze.

A large white beast with massive wings flew across the sky. It had a tail of fire, with thick black hooves. Its body was long and muscular and had a short neck with fire hair. The face of the creature had a long-pointed horn off the tip of its nose. It posed no threat as it sailed over them. She gazed and marveled at its beauty.

She wasn't quite big enough to put on the baldric, so she left it inside Kyö. She held both swords straight up. They were heavy, but she needed to build up her strength if she was going to be the hero that her mother and uncles thought her to be. The hero that she thought her father would be proud of.

She swung them both downward and dropped one out of her left hand. She growled in frustration. Kyö just floated, watching her. She picked it back up and again stood them straight up, feeling the weight. She swung them downward again and held them pointed outward. The muscles in her firearms burned. She took a wide step back with her right foot and brought the swords up and over her head and sliced downward holding them out to the other side.

She turned her wrists, so the sharp edges of the swords faced outwards and then she swung her arms out to the sides like wings. Her shoulders burned as she held the pose. She started shaking, but she held the pose until her arms gave out and dropped to her sides. She looked at Kyö. "This is harder than I had imagined." She said to him.

"Yes, but you are doing great. In no time at all you'll be a dangerous woman." He said.

Viå smiled. She would love to be a great and powerful woman like her mother. To be a hero and to make a name for herself.

A rustling from a nearby bush made her ears perk up, interrupting her thought. She gripped the white handles and set the blades upon her shoulders, getting them ready for an attack if that was indeed what was about to take place.

"Come out of there, it's not very polite sneaking up on someone!" Viå called out in the direction of the noise, trying not to sound frightened.

Out from the bush was a tiny creature that looked like a person, kind of. It wore clothing, but they were more like rags, really. The holey, long sleeve, button down, dirty orange shirt was far too short, showing off the things big round greasy belly. It had on dirty light green pants with large holes in the knees and wore black boots that also had holes in them, with thick black hair protruding from the toes.

Its face was a greasy tannish lumpy form,

hideous with large yellow eyes that had no eyelids, with small black pupils. The hair on top of its head was just a wiry black clump. The nose was non-existent, just a vertical slit. The creature smiled, revealing tiny, yellow, rotten teeth. The being's hands were lumpy like it's face with gross yellowish, untrimmed, brown stained fingernails.

It looked at Viå's swords and then at her. It moved only it's bulbous eyes towards Kyö. The smile still lingering on the creature's face. "Welcome to Vulnu, a place of dreams. I am Twem'l." He said in a high-pitched voice. He looked at them waiting for their introduction.

"Nice to meet you Twem'l. I'm Viå and this is Kyö. Thank you for welcoming us. We've really only stopped so I can stretch out my legs." Viå mentioned, hoping to get rid of the creepy little creature.

"Come with me and we can have a feast!" Twem'l said, still smiling, and looking at them with those large eerie eyes.

"We're good. We have already eaten but

thank you, kindly." Viå said.

"Actually, I insist that you stay and join us for a delicious feast." He said in a rather rude tone.

Confused by his change of tone and starting to become afraid, Viå gripped the handles of her swords. Danger was on the cusps of the situation and she and Kyö needed to escape. "That's very friendly of you Twem'l and we truly do appreciate the offer, but we must be going, now. Thank you." Viå said slowly taking a few steps towards Kyö.

"Viå, I think you had best get in!" Kyö said in urgency as he opened the side of himself.

The strange little creature, person still had the same smile on his face and just stood there staring at them. Suddenly he vanished right before their eyes. Viå ran towards Kyö in a sprint. Suddenly she toppled to the ground from the weight of something on her back. It was Twem'l.

He grabbed her hair and pulled hard, wrenching her head back. "You're going to taste delicious!" He said joyously laughing as he licked her cheek.

Viå pushed herself off the ground, trying to gain some control. As she got to her feet, she noticed more of the creepy little freaks. They were on Kyö, trying to capture him. A few were trying to bite his orb body but couldn't get their mouths wide enough.

Viå reached back and grabbed the wiry black puff of Twem'l's hair and pulled until the tiny little shit released her. She shrugged him off. He again vanished and then reappeared in front of her. "I like it when my feasts fight back. It makes them taste better?" Twem'l stated and then vanished again.

Viå laid a sword on her back in case the damn thing tried to jump on her again. She listened and watched, waiting. Kyö had lifted high into the air, up and up. He spun himself around, tossing all his riders off.

The little freaks screamed as they fell and made heavy thumping sounds as they hit the ground. Many lay with snapped bones and broken necks. The ones still alive howled in pain. Twem'l was nowhere to be seen.

Kyö landed next to Viå and slid the hatch open again. She quickly leaped inside. Kyö closed himself and took off. She sat breathing heavy. Her first battle but not truly and not her last. Suddenly Twem'l appeared and was on top of her, punching her in the face. She could feel her face swell with each hit. "I'm going to start with your toes, then your feet. I'm then going to continue on upward and with each piece I consume, a little more of you will die until that twinkle in the hazel of your eyes has vanquished." He said and then punched her in the nose.

She felt and heard the cartilage pop. She reached to the floor where she had set her swords and found one. She pulled it up fast and took off one of Twem'l's lumpy hands. He grabbed his arm at the wrist. A yellowish-orange blood sprayed from it covering the inside of Kyö.

"Kyö open yourself!" Viå yelled. The hatch slid wide and Viå kicked Twem'l in the face. He fell backwards out of Kyö. She grabbed the clumpy hand and looked out at the world they were leaving. Twem'l fell and landed until he was just a smear on the surface. She chucked the hand after him. "Kyö, let's get out of her!" She said. The door slid closed and off they went.

That was the first time but not the last she used her swords. Her mind went on to the horde of the dead, a planet that was inhabited by dead creatures. To her and Kyö they were dead but not really. Their flesh was rotten, and their bones were exposed but they were alive. They could think, talk, and mate. When the dead found out they were there, they wanted them to join them and so again Viå and Kyö had to fight their way out, but these dead things could not be killed. She hacked and sliced her way through thousands of them and they just kept on coming. She still gets fleshbumps thinking about it.

She's encountered a lot of trials on their way to Ulderelm and in a way she was glad, for she needed the practice and the mental strength gained to fight the war she was about to face.

"Where do we start?" Viå asked Sagfrin.

"We should find forces to join us, but we need to go to each outpost and encampment to do so. The creatures and humans are scattered throughout Ulderelm, so it will take some time, but I must warn that anyone who would join us are all malnourished and not to mention, heavily guarded." Sagfrin said. "Malnourished means, not properly fed, weak and possibly incapable of fighting but we can try." She added.

"It's a place to start." Kyö said.

Shring

"We have been called Choroac for centuries by the inhabitants of this world but we ourselves are named, Shring. That is what we were first named long ago, before this world was named Ulderelm." The Shring said.

Elkron was puzzled. "Before this world?" He wrote in the dirt.

"Long ago, this world was once named, Retula and my race had stumbled upon an underground palace. It is more massive in comparison to what is built on the surface now.

"A Shring known as Saquo, stumbled upon it one day, while out scouting for a place of safety for his tribe; that was trying to escape another race who was trying to enslave them.

When he had stumbled upon the entrance, he crept down inside. It was dark and musty and still is today.

"He went back to the others and gathered up a few of our warriors, which are our fighting force and he also brought with them a Shring named, Guily, who was a light summoner, to light their way through the dark corridors.

"They journeyed and searched through the entire underground palace and found no one but a lonely corpse, which was preserved from being sealed away inside. On the corpse there was a book, a journal, that he had been writing in.

"Within the text was an unbelievable tale about how the world he was from was coming to an end and how he himself had found the palace and hid there to keep safe. When he watched mountains fall and transform and watched the inhabitants turn to dust and blow away with the wind, he rushed into what is now our home and shut himself deep inside, alone.

"He wrote about how when he had resurfaced the next day. The world had changed. Frightened by the new world, he never came out again.

"When they read the words in the book, they got frightened. They showed it to the head of the Shring. He laughed at it and thought it a rather a tall tale and so the Shring all moved into the massive palace and life continued on and the book was kept safe by Guily.

"After several thousands of years something happened, something that made the book reappear. The one who wrote the book had mentioned something about a glimmer that he had seen, which caused him to believe the world was ending and that was precisely what some of our gatherers had seen one day while they were out collecting goods. It was a blue, purple, and yellow glimmer, as described in the book.

"Reguil, a descendant of Guily had been

reading the book for years and had overheard the gatherers speak of the shimmer. Reguil immediately met with the new leader of the Shring, Tylt. He turned Reguil away but Reguil went above Tylt and started telling all the Shring that their world was about to end. The Shring thought he was mad.

"Tylt had Reguil locked away. Needless to say, our world came to an end and now yours is in danger. Plagued by the creatures of dark. This chaos on your land has hindered us as well. Our gatherers can no longer find goods to keep us alive.

"So, we left our people and came to search for answers and that's when we saw you and your friend run into those strange things that mimic the world around them. Your friend escaped without pursuit towards the light in the sky but since you were the one captured, we figured you were the most important one." The Shring said.

Elkron knew who was the more important one, but he was thankful that these Shring had shown up and saved him and his fellowship when they did.

After the hood was tossed back on the cloak, revealing a Choroac, same as the dagger handle. Elkron was horrified. Two more hooded figures came into the room holding the same daggers in their hands, they glowed bright in the Ever-flame lit room.

They approached the elders and with the daggers, they were somehow able to cut off the manacles. Elkron did not know, why or how, but obviously it had to do with light and dark. After the Choroac freed them all, they ordered the elders to follow close behind. The first Choroac lead the way, while the other two followed behind the elders.

Down halls and stairwells, and around corners, they quickly snuck through and out of Drenchin. The elders wanted to rest but the three Choroac had insistent on them to keep moving, to get as far from Drenchin as possible. How they all managed to avoid being spotted by the throng of roaming

Molgren's was an act of the gods.

Now they were up in the North part of Ulderelm in a dense forest named, Blistle woods. Everything was soaking wet from the mist and the lead Shring made a small fire, where they all sat around it.

"What are your names?" Elkron asked wrote.

"I am Sirium." The lead one said. "and that is Tyhim and Harphrum." He said pointing.

Tyhim was a male who was slightly smaller than Sirium and Harphrum was female and very petite. For the most part they looked similar in appearance. Each had shiny dark brown scaly heads and faces down into their collars, with large black eyes on the sides. Their ears were just holes that sat back behind their eyes. Their faces were long with a snout that had little points over their nostrils. Their jaws were thick and wide, with mouths that looked like they could unhinge and probably swallow each elder whole.

Elkron could see little pointed teeth when they spoke. He wondered where their scales ended since their legs were like a human's. The Shring wore gloves and long-sleeved shirts so he couldn't see their flesh beneath. Their half pants went just below their knees, so he was very curious about the depth of their scales. They all wore the same attire. The thing that truly proved that Harphrum was female was because she sounded like one.

If you saw one and then another, you would believe it was the same being. Which was probably why they seemed so elusive. The art of deception!

"Why are you covered everywhere but your legs?" Framen etched into the dirt.

"To give the appearance of man." Harphrum answered.

"Our scales cover are entire bodies until mid-thigh. It makes it easier for us to blend in." Tyhim added.

"So, before I was captured by the elemental sprites, my companion and I were in pursuit of that fallen star. We or I believe that it may be the one that our creator promised to send us to help destroy the Nightmare. To save Ulderelm." Elkron boldly wrote.

"Creator?! Ha, you believe the creator actually gives a fuck about you or me? We're just a game to him or her, hell, it! This Nightmare you claim that has depleted your world is just more proof that no one cares!" Sirium said, bitterly.

"We the elders have spoken to him and he and the other gods have been stripped of their powers due to the pollution of the purple haze. It has plagued the entire universe. He said that the sole creator has offered to send help and I believe that star was it!" Elkron scribbled with emphasis. "It could be the answer to both of our problems!" He added.

Sirium was quiet for a moment. He poked at the fire with a stick. He looked at his two companions and turned towards Elkron. "This world is finished. You believe the one who is supposed to be sent here can fight all the millions of dark creatures that roam it? That they can kill this Nightmare? There's not enough humans or creatures of light left to fight against the threat are there?" Sirium asked doubtfully.

"I do believe that they can. How many Shring are there? You said your kind has been here long before we came, so you must have a force big enough to at least take out some of the threat?!" Elkron wrote.

"We have not lived this long by being risk takers." Tyhim retorted.

"I'd say that since you've come from your cowardly hole to find answers to your problems, that your race is in dire need of a solution and if you are not willing to fight then you might want to go back to your fucking security palace and rot from starvation! You Choroac are nothing but thieves and cowards!" Grumpy Jupin scribbled in anger.

"We saved your ugly, human faced, winged ass's from a fate, I'm sure would have not been too pleasant!" Tyhim roared as he stood up to face Jupin, whose feathers were ruffled already.

"Stand down now!" Sirium ordered. Tyhim stalked off a little way, facing out into the black of the forest.

"Look, things have changed amongst our race and any decision needs to be unanimous. We know we need help to keep thriving and yes, we've spent years living separate from your world, taking what we need to prolong our existence. Let us sleep on this and we will take you to the Shring palace. If the votes are unanimous then we will join you and if they are not, then you we be on your own and hopefully luck will be with you." Sirium said.

"Outsiders are not welcome within our borders." Tyhim said, eyeing Jupin.

"Times are changing and rules that once applied are now useless. It would seem that when this world dies, there is no do over. No waiting until the gameboard is reset." Sirium said. "Also, do I need to remind you of what laws we broke?" He concluded

Tyhim looked in Sirium's eyes for a time. "No, I know what laws." He answered.

"When we get to our home, I'll have the healers look at that wing of yours." Sirium said to Elkron.

Elkron tipped his head forward as a way of saying thanks.

"What laws?" Framen asked in the dirt.

"Consorting with outsiders, leaving our palace for help without properly getting a unanimous vote and mingling in this world." Harphrum said.

The Shadow

His bone knuckles flexed as he gripped the reigns of the foul beast he rode on. It wasn't a fancy beast, but it accomplished its purpose. He ordered two Molgren's to go out and look for a trail, some sign of anything useful but they came back empty handed.

Obviously, he couldn't depend on such idiots to do such a simple task and he often wondered why the Nightmare kept them around. He wanted an answer to that question, but it seemed pretty clear, they were expendable.

Use expendables for all your work and you never have to be weary of killing your better men. For the most part it was a smart move but not when you needed to get shit done.

The rain was coming down hard, which he had not seen in many years and any sign of anything being in the area would be washed away soon. He unmounted the beast and walked into the tree line. He held the torch out over his head, surveying the landscape.

He tried to imagine a star falling and what kind of chaos it would cause upon impact but there was no sign of that. The mundane beasts assured him that this was about the area they had witnessed. Although they couldn't be a hundred percent sure seeming how they were one mountain range over.

His bone feet pressed into the mud as he walked deeper into the tiny forested area. He wished he was doing what he had been doing, long before the Nightmare was freed and found him. Taking lives. Now, since he has been a slave, he hasn't had the pleasure.

Humans were the best for hunting and killing. They had so many emotions and expressions and he could smell the craving to live on them and it was intoxicating. He could almost remember the feeling of placing his bone hands on a human's flesh and feeling their warmth. He would open his bone jaw and start pulling the life out of them. They would show a whole bunch of emotions during the process and he loved it.

These other beasts and creatures were no fun and often were too easy to hunt. Their faces had but a few expressions and none were as exciting as a human. Now the only humans he was around were all the naked women in the palace and the nightmare kept those for himself.

So many times, he wanted to snatch one up and feel her warm skin and drain her of life. It wasn't fair with them running around nude, teasing him. All the different smells coming from them drove him mad.

He enjoyed living and he knew that if he took one for his own selfish needs, he would be dead, deader than he looked. More consciously dead to be precise. Most do mistake him as being dead but actually; he was not at all. He was very much alive.

The whole human bone structure, that he was made up of is how he has always been when he had awakened into Ulderelm and it was shrouded in what looked like a black cloak but was much more like black smoke, for it had no physical properties. It was used to conceal himself as a normal being.

As far and wide as he has traveled, he has never seen another such as himself. That made him feel particularly special, one of kind, but it did make him feel lonely. He often wondered what his purpose was and just left it alone. There was no point trying to understand such things in life, when one day he would be gone. So, he just said, "Fuck it!"

When the Nightmare summoned him to duty again after being free from him during the Nightmare's imprisonment. He had been feasting on the humans of a tiny town, known as Gredge. Who were not too happy with seeing their loved one's dead. They gathered up weapons and started their hunt after him.

Although he feared no one, a large gathering of people could ultimately end him. As they pursued him through the nearby swamp, he was easily able to shadow himself from them, elude them in the darkness of the trees in the swamp.

That's when the Nightmare showed up. The large black beast landed in the swamp. The people's eyes went wide with fear. All of them lowered their weapons and turned to run but the Nightmare waved the scepter of tribulation, creating an inescapable wall.

The throng cried out and clawed at the slimy new obstruction in their path. Many of them huddled down, sobbing like infants.

The Shadow snickered, watching the town's folk cower. Then the sound of splashing water drowned out the crying. A whole mass of Molgren's rushed in to obtain the panicked crowd. Manacles were clasped around their throats, each connected by a thick heavy chain attached to a large iron ball.

They were shitting themselves before but now they were really shitting themselves. The Molgren's pulled and beat the people, making them walk. Not being custom to walking in thick muddy water, many of the humans were falling, taking others down with them.

"Shadow, come forth!" The nightmare commanded.

He thought this was a routine round up, to gather slaves but it seems it was much more. He slowly came out of the dead trees that lined the swamp. "Nightmare, it's good to see you again!" The Shadow said. Honestly, he did not mean it.

"Don't play your fucking games with me! You are but a burden on this land and if I didn't have use for the likes of you, I'd simply break your boney body!" The Nightmare sneered.

"Well then, I'm thankful for that! What is it you wish from me?" The Shadow asked, not at all pleased by his new predicament.

"I have gathered all the beasts of the dark and they are all incompetent and ignorant...

"Let's say, fucking useless in the ways of common thinking. I need someone to lead the forces I have gathered, to be my underling. In charge of them all, to enforce my rule.

"If you find yourself useless to the task then I shall have to find another and then the need for you no longer exists." The Nightmare said definitively.

The Shadow looked at the giant ugly winged beast. Without a choice, he accepted the offer.

Further into the trees, just about through the other side, he noticed a few trees had been freshly snapped in half, but the trajectory from which the Molgren's stated the light was falling, was backwards.

These trees were broken by something large. He looked around on the ground but didn't see any foot prints. He walked through the opening, searching the ground for any sign.

The thick grass made it impossible to find any evidence of something being here.

Finally, in a gap in the grass was a print. The print of a Cremhen. One of the elders; the last elder. The print was facing East. It wasn't very helpful, since the Cremhen can fly but that was a sign that the elder was here and it's now in possession of whatever the light was, if the light was anything significant.

He jumped back on his beast and called forth his small dark force and lead them North. He figured that would be the most likely way the Cremhen would have gone plus he also did not feel like heading South into the mountains.

Dire Frustration

"What the fuck do mean they're gone?!" The Nightmare roared as he grabbed the Molgren who had informed him of the mishap and then ripped him in half at the waist. Blood and guts flopped to the floor.

His rage was unsettling. The naked women stood stiff against the walls as the Nightmare tore off heads, arms, anything that he could grab. The chamber room floor was a massacre of blood, limbs and the insides of Molgren's.

His eyes glowed bright blood red as he ran a hand over his thick, black, bald, head; getting the blood off. He sat back in his chair, tapping the bottom of the scepter on the ground, in thought.

He was all riled up from the disturbing news and the pools of blood that poured onto his floor had set him off. He needed a fix. "Come forth, now!" He ordered at a brunette.

She zigzagged her way through the blood and guts. She stepped up on the chest of a Molgren and then another. She made it to her master. He yanked her on top of him. His genital coming to life and finding that sweet spot.

This one, after his ejaculation had conceived. He could smell it when they did. He sent her to where he sends all the ones who carry his next line up of women.

His lust for blood and penetration was a thriving part of his nature. He never had male heirs only females, which was how he kept up on his inventory of never ending thirst and sexual appetites.

The next woman, he drank her blood after he released himself, until she was lifeless. Then he pushed her onto the floor. Her body toppled onto a decapitated Molgren.

These women believed him a god and in a sense that was true. When he chose them, they felt lucky, regardless of the outcome. They were his most prized possessions and loyal only to him. They could come and go if they wished but his scent made them hungry for him, so they didn't stray too far.

It was time to rally up his dark ones and do another full sweep of Ulderelm. These elders had pushed him to his limitation and they were going to feel his wrath. He ordered one of his women to go find Shug.

Shug "was" the leader of the Molgren's long ago and he was fierce and had no restraints when it came to do what the Nightmare asked. That is why the Nightmare only called on him in dire situations, otherwise the world would be in complete chaos and although Ulderelm looked like a wasteland, it did have an order to it.

A while passed since his woman was sent away to retrieve Shug. The Nightmare had used the scepter of tribulation to get rid of the mess. He waved the scepter, picking up the pile of corpses and their insides and with a flick of his wrist, sent them smashing through the wall and out into the land below.

It would be no more than a day and the heap of bodies would be gone from scavengers, most likely Molgren's who couldn't resist the urge to waste food. The chamber door opened and in walked Shug.

His glowing red eyes were focused on the Nightmare. His hairy bulky figure rippled as he walked. He stopped before the throne.

"As fast as your kind is, I wonder what kept you?" The Nightmare said, questioning the Molgren.

"My lord, I was in the pits punishing the horde for the joys of my own amusement." Shug stated in a growling voice.

"Play time is over. I have a job for you and I want you to take two hundred of the dark ones, then I want ever rock turned, mountain crumbled, lake and river drained, every forest burned until you find every last elder!" The

Nightmare said in a mellow but very serious tone.

"It is done!" Shug said and was gone before the Nightmare even blinked.

He stood up from his throne and paced the room to stretch out his massive legs. Sure, he could go out and destroy the land himself and succeed in finding every elder but what would be the point. He was ruler of Ulderelm and that couldn't be any truer, given who he was; who he truly was. Searching the land was a job for his creatures of the dark.

First Blood

Viå and Sagfrin gazed out over one of the many slave encampments. This one was metal working, where the Nightmare had a race called Rharv's, who were the best metal craftsmen in Ulderelm. The Nightmare had all armor and weapons fabricated for his Neanderthal forces, here. It had always been a place for fabrication and the Nightmare continued to use it as such.

Sagfrin figured that this was the best place to start since they worked with heavy orb and raw materials, which would suggest they were still in somewhat physical condition. The other assumption was they may have manufactured weapons for themselves to free themselves one day. She knew she would if the tools were at her "hands" all day.

"So, are you ready to start a war?" Viå asked Sagfrin mentally so they wouldn't be heard.

Sagfrin looked at her almost distant and nodded. She had not really ever been in battle before. Once when the chaos began she did have to fight to try and save her city but honestly it wasn't a war. She and the other elders had left before they were no longer able to do their duty for Ulderelm, which was to help the savior.

That was their main concern. If they died in their fight to protect the population of Ulderelm then they felt like they have failed. Getting the savior was what they felt was their main objective. For the good; as a whole, for Ulderelm.

"Taking out this post is surely going raise questions and bring more of the Nightmare's men. I need to know if you're ready to handle that?" Viå asked Sagfrin.

"I'm ready." She said confidently. She had

to be strong; for this girl was taken from her family to save Ulderelm and if she was ready to fight and die for the freedom of a world she had just arrived at, then she knew that she had to be ready to do the same. It was now or forever hide and let the Nightmare rule and she was finished hiding.

Sagfrin turned to Viå and waved a wing over her.

"What are you doing?!" Viå asked curiously.

"I'm placing a shield around you, so you will be less vulnerable from attacks. It won't last long but it will be an extra precaution in case of an overwhelming attack that you may not be prepared for." Sagfrin stated.

"Thanks." Viå said. "Kyö, are you ready?" Viå asked.

"Always!" He confirmed.

They had Kyö stay as far back as possible, so his glow did not alert the Molgren's. Even when Kyö dimmed himself to the faintest glow, it still was noticeable in the darkness.

"Let's go!" Viå said with finality.

On Viå's word, Kyö rolled forward from where he was waiting and down the hillside they were perched upon. He descended down towards the outpost of the grounds where a whole bunch of Molgren's; around three hundred were gathered without a care in the world.

Once Kyö was spotted, the ones who noticed him in time jumped out of the way. Three of them were not so fortunate and became one with the earth as Kyö rolled over them.

The Molgren's were very fast and if Viå wasn't part god with certain abilities, she would not have seen them rush around Kyö.

Many Molgren's pulled their weapons but were awe-stricken by the giant orb of light. Kyö increased his glow; so much that the surrounding Molgren's had to squint and that was her time to move. As fast as Viå could, she was down the embankment before Sagfrin even left the top of the hill.

As she raced towards the throng a reality hit

her. She was about to start hacking off heads and poking holes in these creatures and for what reason? What have they done wrong? They have not given her any cause for what she was about to do.

She remembered her mother's message. "In war, decisions must be made to gain the outcome of what you're wanting to accomplish. Even without cause, if you go up against an enemy, don't trust that they'll let you live. You must assume that all on the opposing side will do what they need to in order to gain favor in their leader's eyes." That seemed pretty forward. Kill or be killed. She thought and pulled free her swords.

This will be the first time she actually freed them to draw blood and not to protect herself, but to actually take a life.

She ran around the horde that was distracted by Kyö in a wide circle slicing through the outside group of Molgren's where the shoulder meets the neck.

When she stopped, she stood ready, waiting

for the moment these beasts realized a threat. The Molgren's who she had just cut through started to fall. Heads were rolling across the ground as bodies hit it.

The Molgren's turned to their fallen companions in confusion, gazing at the heads at their feet. Viå blew out a whistle. The beasts turned their heads towards her. Once she was in their sights, their eyes went bright red. They gnashed their teeth, growling for blood.

They charged her in a blur. They were fast, but she was too. She rolled her wrists making the swords loop and held one high above her head and one at mid-waist. They came in fast, slicing like crazy, without any form or thought.

Their jaws were gapping and snapping, as they were trying to taste her flesh. She cut, taking off arms, hands and legs, blood sprayed everywhere. Heads sailed through the air, flinging blood.

Kyö was rolling around trying to flatten any he could. Molgren's were very fast and Kyö, not so much but when the Molgren's were not paying attention, Kyö would run over legs and arms snapping them, on the ones who couldn't escape in time. The sight was almost more gruesome when Kyö ran over a head, making the skull crush, spilling out brains; than Viå cutting open a torso, releasing its contents.

Sagfrin was using the elements to do her damage. She was quick at conjuring her powers. She used them all in quick succession.

She pulled the flames from nearby torches and engulfed three Molgren's, which sent them running wild and ended up taking out several others with them.

Next, she did some strange thing where she created a cyclone that picked up a group of Molgren's and threw them about.

Viå was impressed by Sagfrin's abilities and wished she could do the wonders of commanding the elements. It was something to witness for sure.

In no time at all they had successfully taken out the encampment, leaving not one Molgren left to run off.

Viå wiped the thick blood from her swords off on the thick hair of the closest dead Molgren and then slid them into their scabbards. "Impressive work!" Viå said to Sagfrin. "You are amazing to watch!" She added.

"Thanks. I was a little worried about you myself but seeing how you handled those Molgren's with ease, my faith has been restored." Sagfrin said. "And you Kyö, are fiercer than the Nightmare himself!" She concluded.

Viå repeated what Sagfrin said and he glowed brighter from the compliment and thanked her.

"Let's get in there and free them. We don't want to linger any longer than we have to." Sagfrin demanded. "Kyö will have to stay out here, since he can't fit in the opening." She added.

Inside the compound was completely quiet and dark for the most part. The fire pits were really the only light. Tools and work that was partially finished laid on tables. The water in the troughs were ripple free. The coals in the fire pits still burned.

Viå listened for any sign of life. Breathing filled her ears. There were people here.

"Everything is alright. Please come out, we've come to free you!" She said in a raised but comforting tone.

The sound of chains rattled and dragged as creatures, not people, slowly stood up. Each looked to be plenty healthy but over exerted. This group of slaves needed a good night's sleep.

"You don't have to worry. The threat outside of these walls have been eliminated. We have come to free you. We also ask that you join us in building a force to fight back against the Nightmare and his horde of beasts. Will you join us?!" Viå asked in desperation.

One of the creatures stepped forward, he was quite large but not in the height of Viå but wide and stout. He had one horn on the right side of his head. The other horn was busted off near the scalp.

He had a long scraggly mustache that needed brushed. His eyes were the brightest green Viå had ever seen. His whole appearance was like that of a human man, but he had overly long arms and short stubby legs. The hair on his head was balding and his eyebrows were one with his sideburns.

"Sagfrin. It's so good to see you again. It's been too long! Rumors spread that the elders had been captured." The strange creature said in a rattling voice.

"Translate for me, please." Sagfrin said to Viå.

Viå nodded. "Valcoon, it is nice to see you're doing well, even in your circumstance. It's true the others had been captured, except myself and another elder. We had been in hiding for a long time waiting for the savior to come and when we got the sign, we went in pursuit but got separated and he has yet to return.

"We have been waiting for the gods to send a savior and they finally did. This is Viå." Sagfrin waved a wing towards Viå as Viå pointed at herself. "We are in need of those who want to fight; to take back our home. Will you join us?!"

He looked at his fellow craftsmen and they nodded. He looked back at the two females. "What you see before you is the last of our kind, as far as I've heard. You get these chains off of us and we'll follow you to the end of the world! Vengeance is all we have left!" Valcoon's voice chattered with conviction.

Sagfrin tried everything she could think of to take off the manacle from around Valcoon's neck, but it was no use. Every kind of elemental property she called forth was not the correct alloy. She was getting her feathers ruffled and time was running out. Someone could show up any minute or perhaps have already done so.

Viå asked if she could try her luck at

freeing the manacle. She looked at it, inspected it.

The story Valcoon told them about how they had tried everything to get them off and then told them how they were put on and none of it made any sense. They simply touched it and it latched on but if that were true then there would be a break in the collar but there was none.

She put her hands on it feeling it. She closed her eyes. Her mother had told her that she may possess certain powers such as she did. Her mother said that she could control people and things with her mind as long as it had energy running through it.

Viå tried to go into the collar with her mind but had no luck. Viå often wondered what powers she did possess, if any. During her travel she had tried to reach for a power. Trying to find what she was capable of, but nothing had ever sparked within her. Why would this sole creator choose her, if she did not possess some kind of internal strength?

This time, she truly focused, she didn't try to go into the object; she felt the object, touched it with her thoughts. Felt what it was made of, made with. Although she could not name the elements, there was one thing that she knew very well and that was darkness.

It was the one thing within the collar that was different, and she knew it didn't belong. She focused on that alone. She touched it, pulled at it, shifted it. It was strong, consuming but she had it, took control of it. Something in her clicked and it was very obvious, the opposite of dark is light.

She saw her mother's beautiful face, her blue diamond eyes, and her brilliant smile. Although she was somewhere on the other side of the universe, Viå knew that her mother was waiting. Viå smiled at the thought of hugging her mother again, holding her, hearing her voice. Tears of joy rolled down her cheeks.

The darkness that was fused within the collar had vanished and the thoughts Viå had of her mother left an imprint of dazzling light in its place, making the manacle fall free.

Viå felt with her mind the other manacles all at once and with less effort replaced the darkness with pure light, pure joy. Viå knew now what her power was and that was turning good, beautiful thoughts into pure light energy.

Sagfrin was beside herself. "How did... What did... How in the world?!" She said flabbergasted.

"I don't know really but these holds are powered by darkness and I placed pure light into that space, replacing the darkness and they fell off!" Viå said.

"Interesting. I think it's time you and I had a much deeper talk." Sagfrin said.

Shring Palace

E lkron thought the blindfolds were a bit ridiculous, being an elder after all. They were leaders to Ulderelm, over all the inhabitants of their villages and cities. They were the peace keepers and makers. They were the ones who made laws and the upholders to those laws.

Since this race was supposedly here prior to his and the other elders, he did what they wanted. They did in fact need allies and if Sagfrin did find the savior, that savior would possibly need all the help they could get. This was an opportunity to get the forces they needed.

If they could persuade this race to fight for freedom, then they would next have to try and find Sagfrin. Where; was the issue but that problem was for a later time.

The sound of a door opened and Elkron was gently lowered down, not to disturb his broken wing. "Take a step back. Okay, now wait." Sirium said.

After a moment the sound of the door closed. The blindfold was removed from Elkron's eyes. He looked around the musty room. Torches lit the room they were in. It was a large open room. Paintings hung on the walls of Shring. To Elkron they all were similar, but he knew to the Shring that the ones in the paintings were significantly different to them. In the far end of the empty room was two doors, where Sirium led them.

"I'm letting you know now that the Shring may be hostile and angry that we have brought outsiders here, so stay together and stay close. I'm not sure what they will do, most have never been around those from the outside." Sirium said very seriously.

He knocked in a pattern on a door. The door

clicked and snapped as locks were being turned. Then they opened inward.

The next room was larger than the first and filled with Shring going about their business. That was until they saw the elders. Then they stopped and ogled at them.

"Can I have your attention, please!" Sirium called out. "Please pass on that I need every male to gather here, now. Thank you." Soon those who stood gazing had all rushed off to spread the word.

"This will take some time for there are many." Sirium said.

The room started to fill up with Shring. As the elders and the three Shring stood opposite of the ones piling in, whispers and scowls came from those arriving.

Soon the Shring began forming rows and columns as to fit the Shring still arriving. Not long after, the strangest thing Elkron had ever seen started happening. The Shring began climbing upon each other's shoulders two high. It started in the back of the room and worked its way almost towards the front.

"All here!" The massive group said as one.

"Thank you all for coming!" Sirium said, looking out over the crowd. "As you've already heard and noticed, there are outsiders here. These are the elders, which were in charge of the world above, before a beast that is called the Nightmare took over.

"Just to keep your worries at peace. We blindfolded them, so they would not know of our location and we will blindfold them out of here as well.

"As many of you know, our supplies are no longer capable of sustaining us. We all will dead within the year. That is a problem that we all face and since we live secluded from the rest of the world, have not heard the news.

"We are, as far as we know the third Genocide and soon we will be known as the fourth and there will be no future Shring. This Nightmare has taken over the land and has made it scarce of a future for anyone but himself and his followers.

"They are many and they are ferocious and deadly. We are safe here but here we all will die, our women will die, our young will die. There is an answer and as you know we don't do anything unless we make it unanimous. I have asked the males to come, not to say the females are not capable but as our race goes, we seem to be stronger and we need the power.

"The answer to our problems is to fight. To fight to save our future, to give us a chance to live through a fourth genocide and a fifth and so on. If we don't do this then we die for sure, so I shall give you all a moment to decide our fate." Sirium said, standing stiff and tall.

Elkron now knew that Sirium was the leader of the Shring. It was obvious in that moment. The way he spoke and held himself, was now too plain to see. Being in charge his whole life, he wondered why he didn't see it before.

"How do you know that this Nightmare is the reason for our downfall?" A Shring shouted out.

"It's more than obvious since he's the one who runs the land. Outside these walls, all whom used to walk the earth are no longer visible, for they have been enslaved into encampments throughout the world and you have to travel far and wide to find them. This place above is now a desolate wasteland, where only those who would enslave you or kill you roam. So, I ask you again. Will you fight for our future or spend our remaining days here to die?!" Sirium said sounding somewhat agitated.

Murmurs spread throughout the throng. It went on for a long time and when it would quiet down, anticipation would build, only to be thrown back into more waiting.

"I could have our healer look at that for you, while we wait?" Sirium offered.

Elkron shook his head no. He needed to hear the outcome. His wing has been busted for a while now and a few more hours wouldn't hurt it. Maybe.

"So... A few things." A Shring said. "What

makes you think we can take on these creatures, what do you think we can do?" He asked.

"I thought the same way!" Harphrum spoke up. "I thought that as well until we had watched an outpost and these beasts are nothing more than numbers. They lack any sense of combat. We have our impenetrable scales and our unique way of fighting. This horde outside of these walls are easily brushed aside, I assure you. Most of us, in this room could possibly end this chaos. Also, we have these!" Harphrum held up her white dagger over her head. "With these, we were able to break into a palace and free these elders by the power of these daggers! I believe these may have the strength to help with turning this land around!" She added.

The murmurs spread throughout the crowd again. Elkron eyed Sirium and Sirium turned towards him and the others.

Elkron wondered where they had gotten the orb to make the daggers. He tapped the handle and motioned with his wing.

Sirium stood in thought for a moment trying to understand and then he nodded. "First a drink for us all." He said and called over one of the Shring and from the size, Elkron thought it to be a young one.

Sirium turned back towards the group. "Not too far from here our scavengers came upon a large depression in the ground and these white rocks, more of a metal, were protruding from the ground within the depression. They thought them to be interesting, so they brought them back here.

"We didn't quite understand what they were but in the dark they glowed. When we realized that they were an alloy, we went to work into making these dagger's. When we found you was the first time we had tried to use them other than their intended use, our protection.

"Which I gather you must have been under the same idea of how they work." Sirium explained.

The daggers were holding in the power of

light. A large depression? Elkron wondered but was not quite sure since these daggers were white but maybe... He gestured to Sirium if he could see the dagger.

Sirium was a little hesitant but handed Elkron the blade. Elkron set it on the ground. He started to pull through it, to find the properties. He looked at Sirium and then turned to the elders.

Elkron's suspicions were correct but how? These daggers were made of the Greenite from the mine which held the power of light the elders had placed within them to keep the Nightmare trapped.

He couldn't understand why they glowed white or how they came up to the surface. Elkron gestured a writing motion to Sirium who quickly got the items together.

A hard chunk of a soft red mud or clay was handed to Elkron and a large piece of cloth. The three Shring stood on the corners of the cloth, watching.

Elkron explained what the daggers were

and asked how such a thing could be possible. The other three elders stood in thought as did the Shring.

Tyhim spoke. "What if the power you put into the Greenite changed the elements within it over time and perhaps the reason for them protruding is the same reason things grow and bloom. Maybe the light was trying to find light?" Everyone looked at him.

It did make sense and that could have also been how the Nightmare could conjure up the elemental sprites. Perhaps the Greenite had begun to surface during the time the nightmare was imprisoned, allowing him to gain some of his strength back. Elkron wrote his thoughts down.

The other elders thought for a moment and nodded, that perhaps that's what happened. It really could be the only theory. The only one that made the most sense.

Jupin grabbed the red clump and scribbled: "You're not as empty-headed as I have mistaken you to be, Tyhim. Good job." The elders were wide eyed. As far as they knew that was grumpy Jupin's first complement. Tyhim smiled and patted Jupin on the back.

In their own world they hadn't noticed that the throng of Shring were all quiet, watching them. An answer waited. Just then the young Shring handed them all a drink, water maybe. Elkron took a sip and confirmed his assumption.

"We have come to an accord. In part of the Shring, we together have come to a unanimous decision with terms.

"First, we want our own kingdom, as we may uphold our own ways and beliefs without interference of the outside world.

"Second, we ask to be involved with all trade routes and we in return shall provide our services to said outside world to prolong our race.

"Third, our kingdom shall be access granted only, to keep the Shring palace a secret.

"Fourth, we ask that you four elders forget that you know, seen or heard of this palace.

"As speaking for every Shring here, we agree to help but after which if our spoken contract is bctraycd, a ncw war will start, and we will take over this entire planet." The Shring finished with a half bow and the whole enclave stood awaiting confirmation.

The four elders stood in a line and they all bowed before the entire Shring race, giving them thanks, and agreeing to their demands.

War was about to arise and Elkron hoped Sagfrin had found the savior and that they will join in union before things became chaotically out of hand.

The Birthmark

With fear of being pursued and not wanting to risk a fate that would be inevitable so soon without sufficient man power; Viå, Kyö and Sagfrin led the group out into the mountains, which was by far not a short journey. The mountains were the same ones that her and Elkron had been hiding and had their encounter with the elemental sprites. Sagfrin thought it was best to keep to the valley.

As Sagfrin had guessed, the Rharv's did make weapons and had stashed them in the bottom of the coal storages. Not only weapons but armor too. Each of them was a very skilled in their work, naturally skilled. Their armor looked amazing, like they were actual warriors.

They gloated about the strength of their armor and weapons, since they were made from Greenite, which was unmatched.

Down in a narrow valley, which was basically two rock walls on both sides. They stopped for some rest and with the little food they had taken from the outposts, ate.

"So, do you know what the Nightmare has as far creatures and beasts that I need to be aware of?" Viå asked.

"There are other creatures but as far as I have seen it's just the sprites and the Molgren's. I have yet to know whom else has joined his cause but if he has not yet brought on this creature known as the Shadow, then we're just dealing with the latter but if the Shadow has joined then I'm not too sure if it's more threatening than the elemental sprites." Sagfrin stated.

"Do you know what this Shadow is capable of?" Viå asked.

"Only that it sucks the life out of the living.

I'm not too sure if it can be killed, since the rumors say it is entirely made of bones; human bones." Sagfrin said as she fluffed her feathers around her face.

Since the land has been stripped down, finding more to eat was hard to come by. The beasts that use to roam have been just about exterminated. A few of the group wanted to try and find something more to eat anyways.

Sagfrin had told them to be cautious for their lives were in danger since their escape had probably put a search out for them. She wanted to order them to stay put but they have been locked up in that encampment for many years, so she reluctantly agreed.

Kyö dimmed himself as to not draw too much attention from any outsiders that might happen to see his light from inside the crevice. He was fast asleep after they had stopped.

Sagfrin wanted to know more about this woman who had been stripped of her life and thrown into this one. This woman who can call forth light and replace the dark. "So Viå, I think it's safe for you to tell me your story now." Sagfrin said.

Viå paused in the middle of chewing some dried meat. She looked Sagfrin in her eyes as she swallowed.

"I'm from a place called Buriece and from what I can remember it was a beautiful place. When I was just over a year old, Kyö had come by the order of the sole creator.

"The creator said that I possess powers that could potentially end this darkness that clouds the universe but until today, I've had no luck in awakening this assumed power.

"Within Kyö, whom has the ability to absorb information, has my mother and uncle's last statements and guidance's, so I have some help on this voyage. I play them back from time to time. It helps me when I'm having a horrible day, or I just need information.

"Seeing their faces and hearing their voices calms my center, helps me to be strong. I look forward to the day, that I get to see them again.

"My mother is a beautiful woman and as my mother says, my father was very handsome as well. He's was an Ördük, which are a giant size people on Buriece. My mother is a half god. Which makes myself half of my father and mother." She said with a bright smile.

Sagfrin interrupted her. "God, like the ones who create?"

"Yes, my grandfather was mortal, and my grandmother was a god and from what my mother said, was that my grandmother gave up her place with the gods to be with my grandfather.

"That's pretty much everything minus a few long mundane details." Viå said, rubbing her arms, trying to warm them up a little.

"One more question?" Sagfrin asked. "What is that blue mark on your wrist?" She asked looking at it.

"It's my birthmark; I was born with it. My mother has one as well except it's much different and it's on her chest." Viå said and used a finger to etch it in the soft dirt. "She said that in a time of great need, does it activate. It is apparently the source of my powers. She told me a story about hers when she was at war with her brother Kråg, who had one as well. Identical birthmarks on fraternal twins.

"She mentions that only when she was at her most desperate place in her heart, where she wanted nothing more than for things to be at peace, did she see the answer.

"She freed her mind and forgave her brother for his wrongs. Once doing so, that ignited her birthmark and her brothers at the same time, the reason is unknown. She was then able to take control of the powers inside and will them to her own, both his and hers.

"A dome of white light engulfed them. She had created a physical subconsciousness, a shroud around them. She took them both back through time, to an age that was easily vulnerable and persuasive, where she was able to talk reason to him and he was able to see reason.

"She had given him a choice, a choice of life through her or a life of eternal death. He chose to die forever and not burden my mother with his subconsciousness within her.

"After her brother's death she used the power she had harnessed and fixed a broken world, creating peace.

"My guess is that the circle represents the world and the flat line on top is for land and the one beneath is water. I believe she was the binding goddess that was meant to unite everything together and I believe that her brother, my uncle would have had the same fate if his life had gone a different path.

"I've had a long time to try and decipher my own birthmark and what it could mean. From what the sole creator had said, I have the power to potentially end the darkness.

"After what I did with those collars it's starting to make a little sense. I think perhaps my birthmark could mean that I'm the light in the darkness. But if my mother worked as a whole then mine should work the same, which would mean perhaps I have the potential to be the dark and the light. That is my guess but since I can't call forth the power, then I can't be sure." Viå said, lost in thought.

Sagfrin thought through the things she had heard. Viå made a lot of sense and it seems fitting that she would be the one to stop the Nightmare, since light is what keeps him weak but could Viå destroy him? She was after all a goddess but was it enough? Only in time would they know for sure.

The hunting party returned and had with them five medium sized water swimmers. Not really enough to go around but enough to arouse the bitter mood. They made a few small fires, ate, and then drifted off. Kyö was woken and on watch duty with a few others who had taken an early snooze.

The next day they were to set out and journey to another outpost to rally up more fighting power.

A New Addition

After aimlessly searching the land without any such luck at finding the shooting star or the last elder, the Shadow was getting irritated.

At his wits end he had his small horde stop. He sat upon his beast scoping out the land, looking out over an endless waste of death. The Nightmare had managed to strip it to nothing. Even though he kept the useful resources alive, everything else was gone.

The Shadow needed to feed and with all the humans under slavery, the only thing he could suck the life out of was the damn Molgren's and any other beasts found along the way. If they were not already dead.

Their lives were tasteless and lacked the

joys of his hunt. He wished he could suck the life from the Nightmare. Taste his spirit and watch his blood red eyes turn black. He would give anything to see that giant black beast wither away as he sucked him dry.

He could not go back empty handed and the only news he had to give, was that one of the outposts had been eliminated and the slaves were gone. It would appear that someone or something was very skilled.

He found strange marks of something large, that had rolled around flattening Molgren's and also a set of very delicate footprints, that whoever they belonged to was fast; for they hardly left any tracks to follow but the Rharv's footprints were heavy and they lead South into the valley, but the elders tracks were unmistakable and facing in every direction and it left him again without anywhere to follow but he was not too far behind.

Out in the distance he spotted the elemental creatures and if they were still scouring the land for the last elder then he was lucky.

Because if he was to capture the ugly creature first, maybe the Nightmare might conjure a deal with him. A woman for the elder? Yes, he liked the sound of that. A new agenda.

He watched them, the fucking creatures. Even though he had not spent any time around them, he still despised the damn things. Yet, though he feared nothing, these things that mimicked the elements gave him chills, not that he could get them.

With his new plan for a trade in the forefront of his mind, he ordered his beasts to set out, off to the Northeast, in the opposite direction of those blasted elemental things and the Rharv, for he wanted to gather more Molgren's, so his chances to capture the last elder would be easier.

The Shadow rode on, checking outposts and encampments. The idea that the elder was trying to free up the slaves was one that was officially going to bring the Nightmare's wrath upon Ulderelm.

So far, only the metal worker site has been

taken out. The shadow gave warning to the other outposts and encampments to be on the ready for attacks. The ugly, disgusting Molgren's, grunted in affirmation.

Riding across the desolate land, leaving a trail of dust blowing off towards the West. They were almost to the rye fields.

He held up a hand, pausing his horde of Molgren's. He watched the fields, looking for a threat. Everything looked normal. He slowly led them towards the encampment.

Upon their approach, two big Molgren's came out to meet with them. "I'm checking in on every outpost and encampment, looking for those who are against the Nightmare.

"One has already been destroyed leaving hundreds of dead. I'm hoping to intercept the ones who did it and suck the life from them." The shadow said in his multiple eerie whisper.

The two Molgren's shivered and turned away from the creature, backing away slightly. "You may stay here as long as you wish to, if you think they will be coming here." One of

Molgren's said in his grunted voice.

"I've come to inform you to keep a watchful eye out, so you'll be ready in case of an attack." The Shadow stated. "We will be off now." He added.

As the Shadow was falling out, an alarm bell rang. He turned at the noise and then out over the fields. Soon he was seeing what all the fuss was about.

White glowing lights floated in the air, flashing on the distance; he looked closer and he noticed figures were wielding the floating lights. It was a throng of dark figures, heading their way.

"Attack!" The Shadow ordered to his group. "Bring to me the elder if it's here, kill everything else!" He added, while the mass of Molgren's took off in a blur.

From on top of the beast he had a decent view of the battle. The slaves closest of the rushing horde tried to get out of the way but the balls that tethered them were too heavy for them to run. As they were being trampled, their bursting and tearing skin was leaving a trail of blood, guts and what they once were, smeared into the rye.

The two forces met head on. Molgren's were leaving nothing but bones in their path. From his vantage point he could see the slaughter and chaos unfold. The Molgren's had the advantage and then things started to reverse once they got to the ones wielding the glowing lights. The beings under the cloaks started to take out the Molgren's. The Shadow could now see that the floating lights were actually daggers.

The cloaked figures with their glowing daggers were flipping through the air, slicing, and stabbing everything in their path. Anger was already what he felt. Now it was time for him to join this fight.

He jumped from the beast and started walking through the Molgren's, slaughtered and blood splattered, guts spilled and stringed throughout the rye.

He met the first cloaked figure. It came at

him quick, leaping into the air. The glowing dagger flashed towards him. He caught the cloaked figure by the wrist that held the dagger. He looked at dragger. He was bewildered by it. He couldn't comprehend what it was.

He pushed the cloaked figure to the ground. The hood fell back revealing the creature. The Shadow was shocked to see that it was a creature of legend, the Choroac.

He was going to enjoy the taste of this mythical creature's life. He opened his skull mouth and began syphoning the life that the Choroac had lived, all that it was and wanted to be.

The Choroac showed no sign of fear or even tried to struggle against the Shadow, as the syphoning commenced.

Something was not right. Nothing was happening. Furious, the Shadow tried harder, only to be interrupted by being stabbed in the back. The blade went between two rib bones.

Turning his attention to the culprit and

seeing that it was a man, gave him no sense of urgency. Finally, it was something he could take. With a squeeze and a twist, the wrist of the Choroac snapped, making it howl in pain and dropping the dagger.

The Shadow reached for the dagger and instantly his bone hand burned. He held up his hand to inspect it. Where the dagger touched, his bone was crispy and flakey.

In pain and pissed he yanked the blade out of his back and stabbed the foot of the human, that the blade belonged to. "Here's your fucking blade back!" The Shadow said and yanked his burning bone hand off and tossed it aside. It burst into a pile of ash.

He tore the hand off of the wrist he just snapped and placed it on his bone wrist. The Choroac screamed. Soon, more hooded figures were running towards the Shadow to protect their fallen comrade, so now his human would have wait.

The glowing dagger's were coming in fast. He reached down and grabbed the dagger with his new appendage and leaped back, away from the charging Choroac. He ran for his beast and took off, leaving his horde of Molgren's to their fate.

Pitiful Situation

Elkron's wing was stiff but healed. He continued to rotate it, trying to loosen it. After the Shring agreed to fight, Sirium led Elkron down to the healers. There were many of them. They all wore white cloaks and clothing. Elkron wondered why so many were congregated into one area.

Sirium said hello to all that passed until they got to the end of the room, where Elkron was introduced to Rochi, who was the main healer.

Rochi looked and felt his wing. She closed her eyes and then took away her hands. "All finished." She said.

Elkron was confused. He moved his wing and there was no longer any searing pain.

Remarkable he thought. He wondered if these healers would be joining them in battle, because they would be very valuable. Elkron thought that they would obviously need to change their attire to blend in, so they wouldn't make for easy targets.

When Elkron asked Sirium about the healers joining them, he said that some of them would and that made Elkron feel more at ease about the battle coming.

The idea was fairly simple, find encampments and free the slaves, while taking out as many of the dark ones as possible along the way. It really was the best plan since going straight to Drenchin was a losing battle. It was best to start from the outside, in.

Elkron knew of only a few encampments and the proper one to start with was the slaves at the metal workers outpost but not knowing where they were, that one would have to be placed on hold until he knew of their location and then they would need to work their way in that direction. Unless they happened to be nearby.

So Elkron, after being lead in zigzags and circles in a blindfold, so the location of the Shring palace would remain a mystery was finally able to choose their first outpost. After the blindfold was removed, he looked at the landscape and the closest one nearest to them was the rye fields.

The rye fields were one of the resources used to feed the slaves throughout Ulderelm. Since they were going to free the slaves that would put a hold on production, but he figured they probably had enough food stored up in every encampment, so taking out this encampment wouldn't really hurt. He hoped.

Elkron and Sirium watched from the tree line that looked out over the fields. The slaves were all human and were working endlessly cutting down the tall grass and bundling them up and then loading them onto a cart that was attached to a Whallop, which was a large hairless work beast with thick brown skin. Its head was tiny compared to the body, with oversized twisted horns that grew out the base of the skull. The neck was pretty much one with the body. It was a stout muscular beast that had large flat round feet.

They were the strongest things in Ulderelm and very gentle. The biggest problem with them was they liked to eat everything, so their mouths needed bound unless it was time to feed them. This one was past the point of being healthy and on the verge of death.

The workers had the same look about them as well. Elkron wondered if they could or had any fight in them. He hoped so or this was all for nothing since their main goal was to increase their forces.

Honestly, it was what he was supposed to do, what the elders were supposed to do. To fight and keep Ulderelm safe. So, in a way it would still be for a cause, if they couldn't help battle.

On the other side of the fields, in the distance. A group was approaching. They were so far away, Elkron couldn't quite make out the figures, in the low light of the haze.

It was time. They couldn't stay in the trees forever. Waiting was no longer the answer. Death was now a better option than slavery.

They walked out into the rye, keeping low. When they got near the closest human, who was around mid-twenties, he had spotted them, but quickly averted his attention elsewhere and continued to work, swiping the blade through the tall grain.

Sirium and the rest of the Shring had put their hoods up on their cloaks, to conceal their image, so they didn't frighten the workers.

The elders had no need. The majority of the population knew who they were, and they must be fucking pissed from being let down. Elkron was a little timid about asking the slaves to join them but in reality, it would be Sirium doing all the talking.

"We're not here to hurt you, so don't be alarmed. We're here to free you all." Sirium mentioned.

The man paused momentarily, then went

about his work.

"I am truthful with my words. I would like to know, if you all can and would join us in fighting back against those who keep you enslaved?" Sirium asked.

The man kept swinging the blade. Sirium thought it was a lost cause until the man spoke. "I'm sure if you could free us, most of us would fight." The man stated.

As frail as the man looked, his words sounded honest. Sirium told him to crouch down and then pulled the white dagger from his belt. He touched the blade to the collar around the man's neck. It fell to the ground.

The man felt around his neck in disbelief. Tears filled his eyes. "I've been wearing that thing since I was a boy. Please free the others." He said earnestly.

Sirium motioned for his people to go around to each of the slaves and remove their bindings. After a few conversations, the manacles were thumping to the ground.

This had gained the attention of the monitor

and he sounded an alarm.

All four elders stayed close as the Molgren's came in a blur, all they could see were their glowing red eyes. They all placed a shield around themselves and a few of the Shring.

Being in the rye fields, there was not much of the elements to use in defense, except air and the earth. The Molgren's came in with mashing teeth and weapons drawn.

Elkron pulled up the ground, under foot, tossing a couple of the fast-incoming beasts. Jupin, used an air wisp sending one Molgren flying into an advancing group, who tried to avoid being struck, only to be thumped in the face, snapping the neck of one.

Framen and Piko worked together. Piko was pulling up rocks beneath the surface and Framen was hurling them with an air wisp. Most of the Molgren's didn't even notice what was going on until a rock pelted them through their think hairy flesh. Only a few of the sailing rocks proved fatal, when entering into a Molgren's skull.

Elkron watched the Shring do their thing and damn if they were not good at it. It was hard to not be distracted by the flash of glowing dagger's, buzzing around the fields.

The Shring were flipping and jumping all around the Molgren's. As fast as the Molgren's were it didn't seem to hinder the skills of the Shring. Every cut, strike was executed perfectly. One Shring closest to him had leaped upon the shoulders of a Molgren and took its head clean off with one quick slice and then rode the beheaded Molgren to the ground and then the Shring drop kicked the head into the back of another Molgren.

The Molgren grabbed its head and turned around. It growled and then charged. The Shring stood ready and in a flash of glowing white light the Molgren was split in the side. The power in the dagger turned the Molgren to ash. Its body fell to the ground and shattered, blowing away with the wind.

Elkron hadn't been paying much attention

but now he noticed that the whole field was covered in what used to be Molgren's. The power of the light within the Shring daggers was powerful, thanks to the elders.

A scream of sheer pain came from somewhere out in the distance, Elkron and the other elders followed the sound, along with the Shring.

Out in the distance was a figure with a black cloak that was over the top of a Shring with its hood off. Next to them was the man they first encountered and had freed.

The screams came from the Shring on the ground because the black hooded figure had pulled off its hand. The oddest thing occurred. The cloaked figure placed the Shring hand upon its own nub, its bone nub.

The figure leapt high into the air away from them as they charged. It leaped onto a Borix and trotted off towards the West.

On the ground was Tyhim, blood oozing from the ripped off wrist. "That fuck... broke my... wrist!" He shouted through pain. "Then...

Ugh... He tried to grab the dagger... Mmm... His hand... Fuck!" Tyhim yelled, holding his torn wrist.

"Just relax, the healer will heal you." Sirium said.

A healer, cloaked in white knelt beside Tyhim and placed her hands on his wound. A second later and it was healed. No hand but the break and ripped skin was smoothed over, leaving a nub.

"That bone creature stole my hand! What was that thing? It was stronger than me, than a Molgren! First it had its bone jaws open, looking like it was trying to suck the life from me, then he came and stabbed it and then it stabbed him and then ripped my hand off and stuck it on to itself!" Tyhim said, clearly in panic and had pointed at the man.

Elkron scribbled in a bare spot in the field. "The Shadow!" Everyone read the words.

Blood of Resurrection

The Shadow was face first against the wall. His bone cheek was scraping against the coarse surface. The Nightmare's hand had a grip on the back of the Shadow's skull, pressing it into the wall, almost to the point of it cracking.

"Tell me why I shouldn't shatter your head or grind it to dust?!" The Nightmare asked in a deep, quiet but murderous tone. "Your existence is futile, and my patience has all but retired. I believed that you would have been my wise choice and it would seem that I was wrong." He concluded.

"Just give me a moment to explain. I've got more information for you. If you were not so quick to anger, I could have eased your mind, my lord." The Shadow said, regretting his remark.

The Nightmare let go and the Shadow fell to the floor. He slowly got up and turned to face the enormous black, thick skinned nightmare.

"Oh, great Shadow. I do apologize for being so forth coming in wanting to end your life. My actions were out of line and on the border of immaturity. Will you ever forgive me?" The Nightmare said.

The Shadow looked at him dumbstruck, clearly, he was being sarcastic. The Shadow almost laughed, seeing this enormous creature act sincere. He stood on dangerous grounds. The Shadow quickly dropped to his face, in a fetal position.

"Forgive me, for I know not my own trespasses. My thoughts get away from me at times." The Shadow said in reverence.

"Just get on with what you need to tell me before I kill you." The Nightmare demanded.

The Shadow got up off his face and pulled

from beneath his smoky cloak a folded-up rag and revealed the contents within. He picked up the dagger with his new gloved Choroac hand, which he found to be very interesting and unlike anything in Ulderelm.

"This is the weakness to our strength. When touching it, it turns you into ash. I can only hold it because I tore off this!" He hissed in multitudes as he set the dagger down and took off the glove. "This is the hand, I pulled from a Choroac. It seems that they have joined forces with the elders.

"Another thing; not only did the rye fields get taken over but there seems to be another, a single being who is far more skilled than all the Choroac's combined for they and a single elder massacred the entire metal work encampment and outpost, freeing the Rharv's." He added.

That blade was oddly familiar, and it would appear that there is another being, like the one who imprisoned him the last time roaming about his world. It had to be that falling star or whatever it was. This useless pile of bones before him failed to find out anything truly useful but still managed to bring him information that he could do something about.

He called forth one of his women and ordered her to pick up the dagger. She bent down and scooped it up. Nothing happened to her. In her hands it was an ordinary blade. "Take that and place it over on the table." He ordered.

"When I was locked away, I managed to conceal the scepter of tribulation within the folds of my wings, so I could use its power to escape but the power that the elders used from the sun was too strong for me to use the scepter.

"Slowly over the years, I managed to gain power but not enough. I began to hear voices, inaudible, but voices. I thought I was going mad. The voices continued over the years and one day, I could hear their words. They spoke to me, but I could not see them.

"They were hungry, and I asked what they

could possibly eat, and they said blood. I ripped open my own skin and spilled it on the ground and I was praised for it. Instantly the four creatures of the elements were floating before me.

"It seems that my blood had resurrected these creatures, brought them into this world. In return they offered themselves to me. Blood for a favor.

"I told them about my predicament and what I needed, and they claimed they could get me free from my prison. So, they did. They went out and claimed all five keys of silence and thus here I stand. My blood they drink and my will they do.

"I'm simply telling you this because my reign runs deep in this land and I'm offering you this chance to redeem yourself. You will take my blood from here and place it into the point in which all water flows from.

"From there you will lead the resurrected and all others of mine into battle and annihilate everyone who is against me. You will capture the elders and bring them to me! Is that clear?!" The Nightmare asked and picked the Shadow up by his face, looking into his hollow sockets.

"It is done." The Shadow answered and then the Nightmare tossed him aside, sending him sliding across the floor.

The Nightmare walked to the table where the dagger laid and grabbed a large golden goblet and then bit into his wrist. The blood flowed freely from the tear, the Nightmare placed the goblet beneath the drip, filling it up to the brim.

"Take this and go!" The Nightmare said as he placed a lid on the goblet.

Element of Surprise

A strange sound came from deep in the crevice. They were all packing up when it came. Viå and Kyö were conversing about the best situation to handle the Nightmare, Sagfrin was writing with Valcoon about where to head to next, since they both knew Ulderelm the best.

Everyone pulled their weapons, getting ready for what was possibly coming. Sagfrin and Valcoon rushed up beside Viå and Kyö.

"Beonarf's!" Sagfrin mentally said to Viå. "I thought most of the land animals were wiped out. They usually stay to the forests, they must be really hungry to have come this far!" She started.

Out of the darker part of the crevice rushed

in the Beonarf's. An ugly, mangy creature, with oversized eyes and short wide ears. Their many rows of pointed tiny, drooling teeth were bright white in the dark of the narrow space.

The Rharv's up front were being jumped on and knocked down. Many were hacking away as the threat rushed past. There had to be hundreds of the animal.

One leaped at Viå, she kicked it away, sending it into the side of the wall. Her blades were a blur as she started taking off heads, jaws, legs. She stabbed and cut, leaving a pile before her.

Kyö had no room to roll around and in the crevice, from where they were coming out from was too narrow for him to fit. He could only watch as the rest fought the beasts.

Viå had an idea but she needed the group to fall back. It was a great plan and it wouldn't eliminate all the threat but possibly most or at least half.

"Kyö, can you try and block the way, until I

tell you to move?" Viå asked him.

"Yes." He confirmed.

Viå quickly discussed her plan to Sagfrin who nodded.

"Everyone, fall back!" Viå shouted as Kyö made his way through the crowd of metal workers who were fending off the advancing Beonarf's.

Everyone ran around Kyö, along with quite a few Beonarf's, chasing their intended meals. Kyö rolled over the top of a few Beonarf's and a few of their own into the tight space until only the noses and paws of the Beonarf's were trying to squeeze through the wall and Kyö. A few also tried to clamber over him, without success.

Sagfrin used her powers and summoned the earth of the crevice on both sides and made them collapse inward.

"Move now, Kyö!" Viå screamed, over the growling and whimpering of the Beonarf's and painful cries and yells of injured Rharv's.

Kyö rolled back towards the group, as the

earth fell into the narrow space, landing on top of hundreds of the mangy creatures. A few had managed to sneak past Kyö, escaping their death.

The battle between four legged and the uprights continued until only a few dozen or so Beonarf's were left. They looked at the group with their teeth revealed and mouths drooling, weighing out their options, to continue to try get a meal to stay alive or find something or someone else to consume another day.

The Beonarf's turned and rushed up the only exit out the crevice. The sound of growling and yelping echoed as they got further away from the group.

The casualties were few, but the injuries were great, most were in need of stitches. They bound up those in need and a few thoughts to save some of the beasts for food but the meat on their bones was scarce. It was a wonder how they had survived for this long.

Sagfrin and Valcoon had made up their

minds on the next location and it was a bit of a travel, so the need to locate food and drink were a must along the way. One of the towns that had been destroyed was about mid-way to their next destination and they hoped they could perhaps find some kind of nourishment there, but they needed to be watchful for anything they could eat on the way and collect it but the chances until then was slim.

Kyö floated beside Sagfrin and Viå. Valcoon walked close behind, followed by the group of metal workers, turned warriors.

Although the fierce fight with the Beonarf's was a frightening encounter and a rude start to their day and though they lost a few good friends, everyone was in a rather good mood.

The small group took turns saying a few kind words to their fallen comrades, after they had buried the ones they could get to. These creatures had worked together since their imprisonment and had become close, like family.

Out in the waste land, dust rolled passed.

Sagfrin stopped them, weary that it could be one of the elements. After a moment, she motioned to continue on. With the sprites being part element, it was hard not to be so jumpy.

Sagfrin was curious about this goddess and wanted to know everything but that would be impossible. More so she wanted to know what was out in the space beyond Ulderelm.

"Viå, did you and Kyö visit other places on your journey here?" She asked.

"Certainly, I needed to stop every now and then to find food and drink and also to dispose of my own waste. Also, I needed to find clothing, as I grew up. Not to mention, practice with my swords and sometimes use them. Why?" She asked, intrigued that Sagfrin was interested.

"I was rather curious what those places were like and the things you must have witnessed." Sagfrin stated.

"Most places were beautiful and some not so much. Each had their own distinguished qualities that made them unique. We never spent a whole lot of time in one place, since our main purpose was here.

"I can tell you that we have witnessed some wonderful things but also some dangerous things. As interesting as the places, we visited were they were not as different as here." She said, staring off in the distance.

"I'm curious; how you were able to find us, with the darkness that's spread throughout the space?" Sagfrin asked.

"As I mentioned before, Kyö is an absorbent, meaning he retains information. When he was called upon to help transport me, he was given a map of stars and planets.

"Out there, in the abyss, although shrouded in that purple haze, the planets and stars still give off a glow. Though it is faint, it was still enough to get us to where we needed to go." She mentioned.

"Why can't we see the stars from here? I mean if you could see them from there." Sagfrin asked, staring above.

"I'm not sure, I just know Kyö knew where he was going. He is full of knowledge." She said.

"After you finish your objective here, do you know what you are doing next? Will you be returning home?" Sagfrin asked, looking at Viå.

"I really hope so! That would be a dream come true! I have often dreamt of seeing my mother again, embracing her and catching up on all that I've missed, that she has missed. I hope to settle down and have children of my own one day.

"I don't plan on fighting my entire life. As far as I know I have the "supposed" power to neutralize the darkness. We were sent here because this planet was the most threatened by the darkness." Viå said, tucking a stand of blonde hair behind her ear.

"Have you been to Kyö's home?" Sagfrin asked.

"No but he has shown me images of it. It's very like him. Not in the physical sense. It's not as he puts it, the beginning." She said.

"Not sure I'm grasping your meaning." Sagfrin admitted.

"Well he puts it quite simple saying that places such as this are the beginnings of places like his, the future, where the races are more advanced in creating things such as himself. I believe the word he uses is technology." She said.

"I think I understand. Like the city that I use to look over was more modernized than the rest. We were always making our homes better, our paths better, while the other towns stayed the same, around us." Sagfrin mention.

"Exactly like that, except more advanced. It's hard to fully explain, perhaps when time is more permissible, he can show you." She said.

"So, are there more such as him in his home?" Sagfrin asked, kicking a pebble.

"Yes, many. He said that they come on many colors and not all are lights. He said that the race which made him are very intelligent and that their heads are much larger than their bodies and he showed me an image. He claims they are all that inhabit Cenuu.

"The vision he showed me of his creator was odd. His name was Clypse and his body was a muddy white, with dark veins that ran throughout his body. His head was almost as large as his body, with large opaque eyes, a flat face with two tiny nose holes.

"The most peculiar thing was, he had no mouth or reproductive organs. He had a round belly, with no bellybutton. His arms were long and stretched to the ground, with short legs, kind of like the Rharv's. His hands and feet had only four fingers and toes. Oh, and his neck was about twice as long as mine." She said, touching her throat.

"Was," his creator?" Sagfrin asked, curiously.

"He died of old age." Viå answered.

"How did they eat, without mouths?" She asked sounding baffled.

"They absorb it. They turned their food into a liquid and then take it into themselves." Viå stated as Sagfrin gave her a strange look. "I know, but that's what he said." She added.

"So what purpose was Kyö and his kind made for?" She asked.

"Transporting mainly but with a highly functional artificial intelligence. He was made to think on his own and is filled with the same thought process as his creator.

"He says that the sole creator chose him, since he's more capable than all of his kind, which makes him one of a kind. The few things he lacks are physical emotions and feelings. Like he can't comprehend pain or happiness but he's great at pretending." She said.

"Can he be killed?" Sagfrin asked seeming fascinated.

"I'm not entirely sure; any life-threatening situation we've ever been in, he's never been harmed." She said, turning to Kyö. "Kyö, can you be killed?" She asked him curiously.

"Yes. My internal properties can be damaged beyond repair, where I can no longer function. I can also be brought back, if someone had the intelligence to do so but I don't believe, I would be the same as I am now." He said.

"What do you mean?" Viå asked, confused.

"Simply put, if my memory gets destroyed and someone implemented a new one, I would be different than I am now. It would be like if you were to take out your brain and put a different one in its place. Make sense?" He asked.

Viå nodded. She wondered how strange that would be, to have her mind switched with another, to be inside another body. The idea was mad.

"My outer shell is a composite of magnesium and aluminum, zinc, copper and silicon, which makes it light weight and extremely strong.

"As far as I can tell, no weapon here has the power to break through my shell." He mentioned, glowing brightly, showing pride.

"No worries there?" Viå said out loud.

Sagfrin smiled, which was a first since Viå had met her.

Out in the distance, the small town that no longer exists was nothing but a pile of memories, years of the ones who used to live there sharing laughter and conflicts, raising young ones, uniting together for life, and going about their normal days. There it was waiting for them, a dead town. Its charred structures like an oasis in the distance.

"Border used to be a major import for Clavindar, so they didn't have to travel all the way to Drenchin for goods. So, I'm willing to bet that we may get lucky and find some food transport stashed away." Valcoon mentioned.

"After all this time, do you think it'll still be good?" Viå asked.

"Why would it not?" Valcoon asked. Giving Viå a confounded stare.

"Your food doesn't spoil here?" She asked in general.

"No, we've never had a problem with our

food." Valcoon said.

Viå was very confused. Any food she brought with her along her journey, if not eaten in a specific time would always spoil, always. She let the confusion go and wondered about Clavindar. If it was so far out of the way perhaps there is a chance that were more beings, there that could join their forces.

"So, is Clavindar our next stop?" Viå asked Sagfrin.

She shook her head, no. "Clavindar is deep in the Clavin forest and was the second largest populated city in Ulderelm. An elder named Piko was in charge before, well, you know. The Clavin forest used to be dangerous to travel because of thieves, who had small communities throughout the forest.

"We're headed further North, to an encampment up that way, where my companion, Elkron and I had gone to find food to forage. It's the largest distributer of freshly grown vegetables and most likely the only one.

"Nothing is known anymore, since the last time I was there was years ago and for all I know, it could be gone now." Sagfrin said, sounding doubtful.

"What if there is a whole bunch of creatures, beasts and humans who have hidden themselves in the surrounding forest to escape slavery, when the threat came? How big is this forest?" Viå asked, not letting Clavindar go. She had a feeling about the place, not certain why but it was like it was calling to her. "Listen, I know it's out of the way, but I have a feeling about going to Clavindar, something feels right about it. It's the first feeling I've had and I think we should at least check it out." She said to Valcoon and Sagfrin.

They looked at one another. Valcoon scratched the space between his horn and the busted one. "Let us see what we can find in Border and decide from there." Valcoon said.

Viå nodded. What if she was right, this place could have been avoided all along. If these beings had grown up around the forest, they could very well have secret places to hide. It would also make sense, being the second largest town, that there would be people or creatures still there.

Suddenly the ground shook beneath them. They all laid flat to the ground, shaking with it.

"An earthquake? We hadn't had one of these in my lifetime!" Valcoon shouted in his rattling voice.

"Never in mine either." Sagfrin said mentally to Viå.

Everything came to a stop. They all got up looking around at one another.

"Ulderelm is truly falling apart. Earthquakes are legends that have never been experienced by anyone I know living. Mostly they're written in records as fables." Sagfrin mentioned to Viå.

Viå didn't know what to think. The only thing that she knew for sure was that she needed to end this.

Burnt wood was the only smell that came

from Border. If anything was hidden within a home or shop, it was burned up long ago.

"Look through every place, under the rubbish. Look for any hidden spaces in the floors. It's likely someone could have hidden things in such a location." Valcoon stated.

Kyö hung back on watch. Him being out in the open, in the darkness, glowing as such was a beacon for anyone or anything in the distance. So Viå asked him, if he could roll around in the soot to make his appearance less noticeable.

He did it, but it was not much help, the material he was made of was not wanting the charcoal to stick, but hopefully from far away and with his glow as dim as he could make it, may prove good enough.

Viå went to the furthest home and started moving the ashes around on a table. It was a child's room. There was a picture drawn with chalk, of a strange looking creature with another strange creature upon it. In the background was a sun and two moons with mountains below. It brought back memories of her own pictures that she would draw of her father, mother, and herself. She would put two pieces of parchment together to draw her father. He was the biggest, her mother would tell her. She would put hearts around her father's head. Tears filled her eyes as she thought back to her mother and wished she could see her father.

Upon the table was also a wooden doll that was halfway burned. Its face was kind of freaky looking, with it charred in half. She looked under the table for any kind of hidden spot. Then she looked beneath the bed. Nothing.

The next room offered the same as the last, hiding nothing suspicious. The entire home was simply just that, ordinary.

Over in the neighboring home was more memories of a life gone. In a corner were the remains of two figures, which looked like humans, grasping each other in comfort as their world was set on fire.

Viå could not imagine the terror they must have felt, the helplessness of being without a savior in such a frightening time. All of Ulderelm must have felt this way. Heartbreak filled her. Though she knew that this was long ago, she couldn't help feeling sorrow for these two and those of the same fate. She felt responsible for their lives being taken, even though she knew the time she arrived was the right time. She could not imagine arriving earlier than they did because a year or so earlier and she would not be as confident as she was at this moment.

She knew now was the time to prevent this chaos from happening again, that was why she was her, to bring Ulderelm to peace, to neutralize the threat. She needed to fight for these two gone and those that suffered the same ill fate. She let that give her strength. To push for Ulderelm's future, to be the savior they needed.

"I found something!" One of the Rharv's shouted in its chattering voice.

Viå came running up behind the group. A few of the Rharv's helped move a large burnt piece of a wall. It fell pushing up the dirt, creating a dust cloud. Under a few more pieces there was a door in the floor.

Vulcil, a withered, older Rharv with dark grey hair and yellow-orange horns with a mustache not as mangled as Valcoon's, opened the door in the floor.

It was black inside and without the power of the sun, Sagfrin could not use her powers to create light.

"Kyö, please come here." Viå called out with her mind.

He flew towards her, looking silly with the little ash that did stick to him.

"So far no enemies!" He said.

"That's great news, but I need; we need your light please." Viå stated, pointing towards the group surrounding the opening in the floor.

The group had to break some of the structure that still stood, so that Kyö could get next to the dark space. Once in, he floated above the opening, his light filled the hole.

Valcoon and Vulcil decided to go in. They both climbed down the ladder once they were both down far enough Kyö lowered himself onto the opening. His light filled the space.

Inside, beneath the floor was a wide-open space with a table that was up against the far wall that had a half-melted candle sitting on it. Along the wall next to them was a couple of barrels. Further down the open space was a door.

Valcoon pried open the first barrel with his axe. A strong odor came from it. Inside was a liquid, that looked like water but smelled of fermentation.

"Liquor, I believe." Valcoon said, his voice echoing.

Vulcil pried the other open. "Same." He said.

A noise made them both jump. They turned, weapons ready but the room was empty. They looked at the door.

"Stay close, with weapons ready!" Valcoon said to Vulcil.

They slowly walked to the door, listening for the noise. There was a lock on the door. The only way to see what was inside was to break it and that was going to make a ruckus and alert whatever was on the other side.

"Hand me your knife, please." Valcoon said to Vulcil and switched weapons.

Valcoon slid the blade underneath the lock and slowly pried up. It snapped, echoing through the wide space. The door slowly creaked open. They both took a few steps back, holding their weapons ready.

Darkness was behind the wooden door. It started to open more, creaking as it came did. Out from the black was a young human girl.

Valcoon and Vulcil, lowered their weapons. They stood there in confusion. Where her parents and why was she locked beyond the door? Whom else was going to exit from the darkness? Valcoon wondered.

She cocked her head to the side. She had really long ratty hair that almost touched the floor. Her eyes in the glow of Kyö looked blue. As far as humans go, she was beautiful.

"Where are you parents?" Valcoon asked in his rattling voice. She leaned her head to the other side. "Why are you locked in that room?" He questioned. She stood there staring at them. Things were beginning to get awkward.

"Can you speak?" Valcoon asked her. He looked over at Vulcil and he shrugged. This was a peculiar situation. "Go get everyone!" Valcoon ordered.

"Who is she and where do you think she came from?" Viå asked Sagfrin.

"I'm not sure. If she was locked in here since the towns demise, then she would have been dead. There is food in here but she's not capable of getting to any of it. She remains a mystery.

"I say we stay in here for the time being. We can fill up our stomachs and fill our packs and let everyone get a little sleep." Sagfrin said.

"How old do you think she is?" Viå asked out loud.

"As humans go, I'd say she looks around three or four." Vulcil said.

"I've met three and four-year-old humans who could communicate very well at that age. She seems to know nothing of what we ask or say." Valcoon mentioned to Vulcil.

"The thing that bothers me the most is that door above has not been open since we had opened it, since this town was burned to the ground. That girl has been locked in that pantry since then and has not aged nor died.

"I have a very bad feeling about this. I think something is going on that we have yet not come across." Valcoon said with deep concern in his tone.

"Kyö, we're going to hold up in here for a few hours and let these Rharv's get some sleep. Are you going to be okay for now?" Viå mentally told and asked Kyö as she looked at the little girl.

"Yes, I'll be fine. It's actually quite lovely out here by myself, as I keep you all warm with my undercarriage. Hahaha." Kyö said.

"Your humor, never ceases to amaze me." Viå said. "Contact me in an hour and I'll join you with the watch, so you can get some sleep." she added.

"Certainly." He said.

Viå could only imagine what this girl was going through. Alone, scared, confused. That was how she had felt when she was summoned. When she first set out into the universe within Kyö. Though she had Kyö; it was far from the same as having her family.

This girl being human and surrounded by creatures was probably more scared now, but Viå, looking human could most likely ease the little one's mind. Place comfort in her. All the eerie questions aside, she was a young girl in need of nurture.

Viå sat down beside the little girl. She didn't move. Viå placed a hand on hers. The girl got frightened and pulled her hand away.

"It's okay. I'm not going to hurt you." She said to the girl's mind.

The little girl turned her head to the side and looked up at Viå, through her long hair. The little girl's eyes were very beautiful and blue.

"Do you have a name?" Viå asked, giving the girl a warm smile.

"Dianna." She said in a very childish context.

"That's a beautiful name." Viå said. The girl gave her a smile. "I'm Viå. Can you tell me what you were doing in that room?" She asked.

"Mommy said bad things were coming and said I had to be strong and very quiet. She locked me up. I was alone, scared. It was dark. I was thirsty, hungry. I fell asleep and woke up and I'm supposed to go somewhere. My mind is telling me that I need to go that way." She said pointing North with her child finger. "Then the door opened, and they were here." She said pointing at Valcoon and Vulcil.

"How old are you, Dianna?" Viå asked, curiously.

She held up her hand with all fingers spread, showing Viå her age. It made sense giving how well she was able to communicate mentally with her.

"Are you hungry?" Viå asked flashing her another smile. Dianna shook her head, no. That was peculiar since she had just mentioned being hungry. "Why are you supposed to go that way?" Viå asked curiously.

Dianna shrugged. "My head is telling me to." She said.

Viå conveyed the info to Sagfrin. Sagfrin was very interested and had Viå begin asking questions.

The first was; "What was the bad things?"

"Bad things were coming to take us, she said. I need to hide and keep safe. I heard her lock the door."

The second was; "What do you mean, you fell asleep?"

"I was hungry and thirsty, and I couldn't get

to the food. I was hungry for so long. It was a long time. It was dark. I fell asleep. Then I woke up."

Sagfrin looked at Viå, concerned. Then she said something to Viå that gave her chills. "This young one, I believe has died and somehow been brought back from the dead."

"Are you sure?" Viå asked.

"It's the only thing that makes sense. If she is no longer hungry or thirsty then I'm right. We'll know for sure if she's not hungry in the next few hours." She said.

"If she's been dead since this place was burned down, then why has she not rotted or even smell like it?" Viå asked.

Sagfrin was quiet in thought then she answered. "I believe that being down here and confined in that room has protected her from the elements. I think it being that lack of air has preserved her body. She may start taking on a smell eventually if she is actually dead reincarnated." Sagfrin stated.

"Why do you think she needs to go North?"

Viå asked, hoping to get some clarity.

"I'm not sure. Perhaps whomever brought her back, is manipulating her thoughts. I think we need to watch her carefully. She could be a potential danger to herself or to us. I think it's best if we keep her from going where she thinks she must, for now.

"She seems to not be very strong guided if she's not trying to get out now. She also has her own personality and can form her own thoughts. Ask her how strong the urge is to head North?" Sagfrin said.

"Dianna, dear. How strong is your desire to go to where you think you must?" She asked.

"It's all I can think about." Dianna answered.

All the Rharv's slept hard. Years of being forced into doing slave work had made them exhausted beyond just days of sleep. They needed a long vacation and hopefully after Viå has brought peace to Ulderelm they would get it.

Viå had cuddled with the five-year-old,

Dianna to comfort her and was just about asleep when Kyö told her it was time.

She climbed up the ladder and out into the ash village and sat next to Kyö. She gave him the information of what was happening. He was comforting in the situation. He told her that the girl would be fine and that she would bring peace to the world and the little girl. Dianna would be able to be at rest if she was in fact dead.

After Viå's shift, she went below to check on her companions. Everyone was up and ready to go. Viå had made sure to pack a little extra for everyone, just in case. Kyö made the perfect storage now that Viå was not riding inside.

Viå had told Dianna she would place her inside her friend Kyö and she would be secure there. Clearly, she was confused until Viå showed her. Dianna was more than willing.

Down beneath; the group started filing out. Viå went to check on Sagfrin, who was checking with Valcoon about the Clavin forest and what potential threats they might encounter.

A scream came from above. Viå rushed up out of the hole. Both blades were pulled and ready to make pieces of the threat. The sight before her was a nightmare in reality. She tried to envision what Sagfrin was saying but seeing it was far different than what she had imagined.

Two Rharv's were dangling, five feet from the ground. A liquid like creature had them by their faces. The transparent creature was twice the size of Kyö. The Rharv's were dead by drowning. The thing let them drop to the ground, their lifeless bodies thumped in a contorted heap.

Wind, fire, earth, and water were all around them. These were the elemental sprites Sagfrin had spoken of. The threat was more imposing than she had imagined. What was she going to do? These things had to have a weakness.

The first thing that was needing done was to get Sagfrin out of here. Viå frantically looked for her around the scattered Rharv's, who were waiting for the fight to come for them.

Sagfrin was spotted, ducked behind a turned over table. Viå quickly rushed to her side. "We've got to get you out of here!" She said. "You can travel inside Kyö. You will be safe there along with Dianna. He can take you North and then loop back around towards the Clavin forest." She added.

"What about everyone else? All the work of gathering forces would be for nothing!" Sagfrin stated, her feathers ruffled.

"If what you told me is true, then they're here for you and will follow you wherever you go! It's the only plan we have to keep everyone safe!" Viå said.

Sagfrin looked at her new ally and nodded her agreement. "Kyö we're headed your way. Be ready for another passenger." Viå said, touching Sagfrin on her back.

"Waiting." Kyö confirmed. He was out in the distance, furthest away from the threat.

"Meet me halfway!" She said as her and Sagfrin took off towards Kyö, who also started his way towards them.

Viå picked up Sagfrin and ran, both a blur. Kyö slid his door wide open. Viå who had a hold of Sagfrin, carrying her along, gave her a hefty toss, right into the seat, next to Dianna.

"Fly far North and circle back, meeting us in the Clavin forest!" Viå said to Kyö.

He took off and so did the elemental sprites. The wind was howling as the wind sprite used the air around itself to try and stop Kyö. The water sprite, swung its transparent arm, knocking a group of Rharv's back as it turned to follow Kyö. The fire sprite had done its damage on three of the Rharv's. They screamed as they rolled across the ground. The flames that ignited their bodies was not giving up. They continued to burn, even after they had taken their last breaths. The earth sprite had sent a cloud of dust heavy enough to bury anyone in its path, but it proved to take no prisoners to their graves.

All the elements were now chasing Kyö, who seemed to be hitting an invisible wall of air. The water sprite doused the land with water, as the earth sprite scooped up the mud and started hurling the soggy mass at Kyö, knocking him down.

He caught himself but was in trouble. The fire sprite was sending flames out towards Kyö. Viå needed to help him. She turned to Valcoon.

"It's now or we all die here! Run to the Clavin forest and wait! I'll find you!" She ordered.

"Everyone, head to the forest, now!" Valcoon ordered. The group that was left, quickly grabbed the packs of their fallen comrades, the ones they could get at and quickly ran towards the forest. It was a long way off.

Viå rushed towards the sprites, she had to be quick, for one bad move could very easily end her life. She jumped into the current of air that the wind sprite was pulling into itself. Her swords ready to play, she eyed her target. The sprite was so occupied with taking down Kyö to get at Sagfrin, it didn't even notice that Viå was coming and coming in fast.

The black orb in the center, had a strange electric buzz spinning around and through it. She jabbed her left sword into the little black, electric orb.

The wind ceased as the orb was penetrated. She landed on the ground and quickly swung the sword into the earth, shattering the sprite. It burst into fragments and an electric wisp escaped into the air.

The other sprites were now aware of Viå and forgotten about Kyö, harboring Sagfrin. He flew back, spinning, shedding the now hard clay that had him encased.

Viå dodged a flow of hot flames that blazed past her face. She knew the flames were dangerous and would possibly melt her swords, so she avoided that creature and went after the water sprite instead.

Taking down the water sprite was a lot more difficult than she imagined it to be. First, she lost a sword within it and then she was knocked back, sliding across the dirt, leaving her soaking wet and covered in dirt.

She jumped up and then charged straight into a dive inside the water creatures, grasping her sword along with the sprite and rolled out the other end. The mass of water splattered on the ground, into a large puddle.

The electric pulses of the black sprite, were jolting through her body. She quickly placed the black orb beneath her foot and pressed her weight Kyö, ignoring the plan and thinking the threat was eliminated, was surprised by the earth sprite, who had brought a large wave of mud, crushing him beneath it. Kyö rolled through the dust. The fire sprite was right there, throwing hot bursts of flames at him.

Whatever Kyö was made of, was apparently able to deflect the licking fire. The earth creature had one long arm of solid mud latched onto Kyö. With one up and down swing, Kyö came crashing to the ground, then the process was repeated again.

Viå tried to rush in but the fire sprite had other plans. It came in bright and hot. The white flames blazed at her. How was she supposed to extinguish this flame? This creature would burn beneath water. She would have to trap it in a box without any of the natural elements that keep it burning and still that may not put it out, but maybe enough to reach its main source, the core.

While she thought of the situation at hand, Kyö was still being slammed, repeatedly into the earth. Her friends inside must have been getting pretty dizzy, even with the balance seat within that kept them from flipping around as Kyö moved.

She had an idea and it was her best one. She rushed in a blur around the fire sprite and met up with the earth sprite and cut the arm in half sending Kyö tumbling and bouncing across the ground. Dust filled the air and blew off towards the East.

She started to provoke the earth element by picking up little stones and chucking them at it. It started to push the ground up in quick bursts, causing the dirt to explode upon reaching her.

Her speed was no match for this tactic, but it was a start to her plan. With an ample number of strategies at its disposal, she had to hope it would use the one she needed, or at least one like what she needed.

She kept pushing and the sprite kept throwing various attacks. Finally, the sprite sent a wave of destruction after her and it was exactly the one she was wanting. She quickly rolled behind the fire sprite. The wave came crashing down on top of the fire element before it knew what happened. A mound of thick dirt where the fire sprite once was, had given her an easy target. She quickly began stabbing her swords into the earth until she felt it connect with something hard. She pried her sword up and out of the ground and on the tip of her blade was the damn electric orb. It burst and went with the others.

The earth sprite was no match for her, even with its rock shield. Her speed and swords easily penetrated its surface. She walked right through its attacks and looked it right into its "eyes" and shoved a blade through its black center, killing the impulse.

She rushed to Kyö, who hadn't moved since his tumble. She punched the hard crust off, making it crack and fall away.

"Kyö, Kyö are you okay?" She asked touching him, feeling him. Kyö, don't do this to me!" Viå screamed.

"I'm alive. Just damaged. I can no longer glow for the chemical used has been leaked from my cracked outer shell." Kyö said as he slid the door open. "All within are safe." He added. The ground beneath him had a fluorescent liquid covering it.

Viå knew they were fine for she and Kyö have been in some similar circumstances. Right now, she was concerned for her friend, her companion. He was a brother, he was family. She ran a finger across the crack.

"Are there any terminal effects from this?" Viå asked.

"As far as the analysis shows, this is just a minor fracture and has no internal effects. My beautiful glow is now gone and as far as I know, my home planet is the only place I can be repaired." He stated.

"I'm so glad you're okay! I promise we'll fix you!" She said, hugging him.

"Are you two alright?" Viå asked.

"Not at all how I imagined it!" Sagfrin said, oddly amused.

Dianna said nothing, she just sat there, still.

"Dianna, are you all right?" Viå asked telepathically. Dianna sat motionless. just looking forward.

"Okay, then. Next time Kyö, stay with the plan no matter what! When this is done and over with we'll return to your home and get you fixed." Viå said confidently. "Let us catch up with the others." She added.

Let It Burn

Shug stood with his forces facing the thick forest. He yelled at his Molgren's, ordering them to burn it down. He brought Ever-flame with him and planned on doing exactly what the Nightmare wanted; destroy the land and bring carnage to Ulderelm and perhaps bring the elders to him. He wasn't great at following orders that didn't involve killing.

The flames touched the bark of a single tree and ignited. Once engulfed, it jumped to the next and so on. Any life within would not have time to run.

"I fucking love it! Haha! Destroying things that others find beautiful and pleasant, brings me great joy. It's been too long!" He said out loud to himself.

After several minutes of watching the blaze, Shug was bored. It was time to take off and find something else to destroy.

Not much covered Ulderelm anymore. Shug had mostly to do with that, since he was the one who had burned down every town, city, and village apart from the fire pixie.

His Molgren forces marched the land and invaded homes, raping and stealing as they went. Bones of young and old were stripped cleaned in seconds as they fed.

Those were the days that he missed the most because he had a purpose. Now, he's been confined in Drenchin for so long, waiting to be called on. He used to be ruler of the Molgren's but now he was ruled by the Nightmare.

He used to love the night raids back when they were only confined to it. When the sun of the days burdened them. They would go to villages and he and his horde would do whatever they liked. He would go after the females. He had raped almost every race of female and his favorite was the Rharv's.

He loved the way they kicked and tried headbutt. He loved the struggle. Others had tried to fight him off, but they eventually gave up and cried until he was finished, then he would devourer them but not a Rharv; they fought until the end and he loved it.

Their own race of females was not much fun and most of them were worn out after giving birth to so many younglings and they had no excitement when mating, they just laid there. His five life mates were just for giving birth to his name. Something the Molgren's prided themselves in. The more younglings one had, the higher you were in the clan. He had over thirty; where they were now, he didn't give a fuck.

They prided themselves with many but could care less where they were or what happened to them. After birth they were on their own.

Now, the only females he had were his kind

and he was sick of them. This venture that he was sent on was an opportunity to find some strange.

They had made their way Northwest to an encampment, where they were harvesting disgusting plants that most of the light creatures ate. The Nightmare had ordered to keep the food sources going to keep the slaves alive.

So far, he had seen nothing that would prove that the slaves were worth keeping alive. They basically sustained themselves and were not put to any use other than that.

If he was in charge, there would be structures built in his name, sculptures, shit like that. The Nightmare stayed in his throne room, fucking human women, and murdering them while drinking their blood. Although he despised his leader, he knew not to cross him.

"What slaves do you have of a female nature, my cock needs moistened?" Shug asked the one in charge of overseeing the harvesters.

"I've got a really ugly Rharv hag, that hasn't seen a cock in years and I've also got a few young human ones whom have past the point of being useful to the Nightmare. You know, child birth. They came in about five days ago." The overseer said, snarling.

"Show me there Rharv!" He ordered in his growly voice.

They walked to the fields where hundreds of thin, almost dead looking slaves were replanting the field. He almost couldn't contain himself when he seen her, but he remained calm but, on the inside, he was going mad.

He went out to her in a rush and stopped, standing right behind her, watching as she was on all fours, scooping the dirt and dropping a seed. He was curious as to why she was on all fours when she had short legs and long ass arms. With her being bent down, she was practically begging for it. Teasing him like that. Her ass swayed left and right as she scooted backwards.

He was done waiting, done watching. In a blur, he had her leggings down to her knees and was inside before she even knew it.

She kicked her stubby legs wildly and thrust her head back, trying to headbutt her assailant, who had trespassed her boundaries. "Get your cock out of me, you fuck!" She screamed.

Shug grabbed her horns and held on as he did what he had been waiting on for years. She swung her long arms back behind her hitting Shug as hard as she could. He kept on thrusting. She was going wild and he was riding her like a pro with a big grin stretched across his face.

He wrenched her head back and looked into her old green eyes. "Damn, they said you were ugly, but you are as fucking ugly as they come but your lady parts are real nice and real tight!" He said through growly deep breaths.

Everyone around went about their business, ignoring the scene. They knew better than to get involved or even acknowledge anything but their job.

"Help, get the fuck off, help!" She yelled, through sobs.

Shug put all his weight on her head, shoving her face in the soft dirt. She frantically squirmed beneath him, trying to get air. He continued to force himself on her until they both went still.

"Woah, fuck! That Rharv was a thrill!" He shouted aloud followed by a large toothy grin. He slapped her on the ass and stood, then kicked dirt onto the dead Rharv.

He returned to his audience. "That was fucking exhilarating! Now let's go fuck some more shit up!" He said as he grabbed a torch from one of his Molgren and then lit the small nearby forest on fire. "Let that fucker burn and let's go!" He ordered.

As they were getting ready to leave, the encampment shook. They all stood wide legged, trying to stabilize against the shaking. Out in the fields the slaves held fast since they were already on the ground.

After the vigorous shaking subsided the Molgren's went towards the fields to make sure the slaves continued with their work, but Shug told them to stand down and he would take care of it.

Shug walked out and stood center. He liked being in charge and being who he used to be, the other Molgren's still showed him the same respect earned.

"I don't care what that was or how scared shit you are. Those seeds are not going to fucking plant themselves!" He shouted angrily in his growling voice. "Now get back to fucking work!"

The Resurrected

The point where all water sources flowed from was at the top of Sun peek mountain, which was far North. It took him a full two days, he figured to travel there.

He had the golden goblet, filled with the Nightmare's blood. He wondered what would happen if he drank it but that was a mystery for those who wanted to play with death.

Sure, he could spend his days hiding from the Nightmare and his horde of filthy Molgren's but what kind of life would that be and besides, the Nightmare did somehow track him down, although he had no idea how. If he did leave he would be no longer a slave, he would still be confined to hiding. A losing choice truly.

He took the lid off the goblet and looked inside. The aroma of blood filled his nose hole. He looked down into this place were all water came from. Peculiar it was to him that this round hole, no bigger around than the largest tree he had seen was the source of all water on Ulderelm.

"Bottoms up!" The Shadow said as he did what he was ordered and poured the blood into the burbling waters.

It started to mist beneath the surface, then dispersed. The water began to shift from clear to burgundy, then dark red. The consistency looked to have changed as well, into the thickness of blood.

The now blood water descended to the world below. The whole of Ulderelm started to shake. He held on to a tiny bush next to him. The rumbling ended. He let go of the bush, baffled by what just happened.

The Nightmare's blood was powerful, and he wondered just how powerful it really was. He mentioned that his blood had resurrected those elemental creatures. Now he had to find the resurrected. Where would he look? How would he know?

He began his long trek back down the mountain. His new hand had been acting up since his journey to the main source of water. He moved it around trying to ease up the strange feeling it gave him.

This has never happened before. Whenever he took a new appendage, it worked as well as any of his others. Although his entire structure was made up of used body parts from his many encounters with those trying to kill him but failed, they always had worked.

Eventually those new added limbs would turn to bone, but this hand was giving him problems. He thought about ditching it but then he would have only one hand.

The other thing he couldn't figure out was why he couldn't take the life from the Choroac. The strange creature said to bring luck, but so far, he got nothing but problems.

He had thought about riding the beast he

had rode but he wanted to ponder on things. Walking was the easiest way for him to do so. So, on he went, and it would be a while before he got back to Drenchin if that was where he was supposed to find the resurrected.

"Throw them in there!" A Molgren said pointing to a ditch. It was where they tossed all the dead after they killed over.

Inside the compound the Molgren's were all trying to sleep. A few took turns watching over the slaves as they slept out in the brick yard.

Recently the slaves had been driven harder to produce bricks for the Nightmare, which was making them fatigue and passing out.

The food in the last few years had begun to dwindle, due to the darkness becoming hazier. They were never having problems before with things growing, since what little of the sun's energy was able to penetrate through the darkness enough to feed the crops but not anymore.

One of the Molgren's on watch was making his rounds, when he noticed that one of the slaves looked a little more than asleep. He nudged it with a foot. It didn't move. So, he nudged it again harder, confirming it was dead. He grabbed the slave by the hair and started dragging it towards the dump site.

The ball at the end of the chain got snagged on a box full of wet clay. The Molgren pulled the slave as hard as he could, tearing the slaves neck apart from the shoulder. The cartilage connecting the spine was strong and pulled against the Molgren. He pulled harder breaking the bones from the rib cage, taking the head and spinal column from its body. "Fuck!" The Molgren growled. Now he had a bloody mess to deal with.

He walked over to the ball and picked it up and continued to drag the slave with the ball under one arm and the head with the spine in the other hand, leaving a trail of blood.

At the edge of the trench he tossed the two halves of the slave into it. As he was walking away, the earth began to shake. He lost his balance and fell backwards into the pit, landing on top of the pile of rotting corpses.

"What the fuck?!" He roared as he tried to stand up but the contorted, jumbled mass of death beneath him and with the shaking made it hard to get his footing.

"Come on! This is some fucked up shit!" He grumbled.

After the passing of the earth rumble, he was finally able to stand up. As he took a step, the body he tried to step on moved.

He paused and looked down and the hair covering his body stood stiff with fear. Instantly the black hair covering him turned white. The eyes of the head twisted backwards were open, looking at him with life. The body picked itself up and stood facing him with its head backwards. It reached up and turned it to the front.

The Molgren, scared as shit, ran as fast as he could up and out of the trench; stepping on moving bodies.

When he got to the top he looked down. Everybody, even the one he had just tossed in moments before had come back to life. They all looked around, curious why they were in a pit.

The ones with mortal wounds, touched those areas and wondered how they were alive. The one that the Molgren had tossed in had somehow replaced its own spine back inside itself. The Molgren turned and ran off to get the others.

Her eyes opened to pitch black, nothing visible. She crawled around on the floor, feeling for something, anything.

She stood up slowly, feeling above her head, making sure she wasn't going to hit it on anything hiding in the dark. She put her hands out in front and took tiny steps, feeling the ground with her feet and the air in front of her.

She finally found something in the dark. It was a wall. She slowly followed it, sidling along, and stopped when she heard a sound.

It came from somewhere, where she was not. Was she in a room? Yes, a room. She remembered, that her mother had placed her inside because bad things were coming and then locked the door to keep her extra safe.

She remembers waiting for a long, long time. She remembers, she was thirsty and needed water and food. Her tummy was hungry and making strange noises.

She remembered that she couldn't get to the food above because the shelves were too high for her to reach. After a long time of being hungry and thirsty, she remembered that her eyes closed, she fell asleep.

Now she was awake, but she was not thirsty or hungry. She felt different, somehow. Something was telling her to go somewhere. It was in her head, a direction but she was locked in a room and so she couldn't go anywhere.

The sounds came again but louder and then moments later, a light came into the room. It was faint, but she could see it. It was beneath the door. She walked over to it and stood, listening.

Was it her mom, her dad? Was it the bad things? She listened and heard talking. She couldn't quite hear the words. She went to place her ear to the door but ended up bumping into it with her head.

The next noise she heard was talking. "Hand me your knife, please." It said.

Then she heard scraping on the door and then a loud popping noise. The door came open just a crack, letting in more light. She backed away for a moment. She waited, then used her foot to push it open more.

She scooted away from the light, so she wouldn't be seen. Out in the open room were two Rharv's, she believed they were called. Her mommy said they were nice creatures, just like humans. But the Rharv's had bad things that can hurt people. Perhaps they were scared.

She was not though, so she stepped out of the room and the two Rharv's lowered their weapons.

Shug stood looking around at the slaves. Just having made his threat, the slaves quickly went back to work.

"That's right." He said beneath his breath. He began to walk back to his squad when a noise came from behind him. He spun around and saw nothing. He turned back around, when a sharp pain made him scream.

He looked down and the female Rharv he had raped and murdered, had his cock in her mouth and was pulling hard with her teeth, tearing away his cock.

He watched in horror as it stretched and then started to shred, spilling blood. Panicked, he started hitting the Rharv in the side of her head, trying to stop this madness but it didn't work. Blood started to really dribble from his genital.

Her mouth now was full of his cock. Her face was smeared with blood. She spit it on the ground and then smiled wide and stood up, looking into his eyes.

Freaked, panicked and in shock, he pulled out his knife and stabbed her in the chest with it, but nothing, no scream of pain, no conscience of being penetrated again by him.

His hands on his crotch, trying to stop the flow of blood. He reached down to pick up his cock. It was a wiggling, bloody mess in his hand. He just sat there looking at his dismemberment.

The Rharv, simply smiled and walked off towards the South, knife still embedded in her.

Shag screamed after her. "You're going to pay, you fuck!" He went silent when figures walked past him. Dead figures, a few with heads in hands. Others with guts trailing behind them, pointing, and laughing at the cockless Molgren. He just sat there in shock by the sight as they followed the Rharv.

The shadow made it down to what was known as the Shallows. He heard what sounded like a multitude of people, creatures, and beasts.

When he got out to the wide-open area of the Shallows, his thoughts were mostly right. It was in fact a multitude of things gathered. They were those things he had thought, but they were all dead, resurrected.

He knew they were dead because a lot of them were rotten corpses. He could smell their putrid bodies. They all looked at him, like they were waiting. He honestly was freaked out by the throng.

"What is going on?!" A naked woman asked.

"Yeah, why have we come back from death?!" A male Rharv asked baffled.

"Why are we questioning the Shadow?" A man asked, holding his intestines in, sounding irritated.

"How did we all end up here and why?" An Arglar asked.

The Shadow looked out at the mass. If they were back from the dead but were still able to put together a thought of their own free will, then why did they all meet up here? Couldn't they have gone anywhere?

"Can you tell me, what made you come here?" He asked.

"A feeling inside, made us come this way. Whenever I thought to go somewhere else, I found myself still heading here." A man said.

"Same, for me!" Another said. Soon a collective of voices confirmed that they had all done the same thing.

He looked out over the multitude and stood to his full height. "So, I have brought you all back to life using the Nightmare's blood. You are going into battle against the threat that opposes him. I am to lead you through the land to run over any who are his enemy." The Shadow stated in his multitude of whispering voices.

"What if we choose not to?" The naked woman asked.

"Do you believe you have a choice? You're all here now, against your will." He said matter of fact.

"What about the children? You expect them

to fight. That one right there is only like two years old!" A Rharv said.

"Quit your fucking whining!" A Molgren roared and popped the Rharv in the face.

"Knock out off!" The Shadow ordered and the two froze and returned facing forward.

Obedient these dead were. He was going to enjoy his new position of power for however long he had it.

"The kids are dead and so are you. Your morals mean nothing to the Nightmare or to me! Let us leave now!" He said and approached a dead man, grabbing his hand and then tore it off. The man showed no emotion. He then ripped off the Choroac hand and replaced it with the man's. He then began to walk through the throng of dead.

There had to be close to a couple million or so under his command. As disturbing as some of the dead were, who had been dead for so long, they were nothing but bones like him, but the kids were even more eerie.

He wasn't sure what a crawling infant was

capable of, most likely nothing but the ones who were able to walk would serve well as a distraction. Everyone always seemed to want to help a child. He could use that tactic.

Once he finally made it to the other side of the dead, he began heading South. Where? He wasn't sure, but he was going to run into those elders and the Choroac eventually and when he did, they were going to regret their choice in rising up against the Nightmare.

First, he needed to get the dead weapons. Where was he going to find enough for them, he was not sure.

Clavindar

They entered the Clavin forest, the sound of the desolate land they had left was gone. Now within the tree line, all noise ceased to exist.

Valcoon had everyone rest as they waited for Viå, Kyö, Sagfrin and the little girl Dianna to join them. They all sat down in a clearing just off the main path.

It being so long since the Nightmare has destroyed the land, there was no telling what may use the paths now.

Valcoon has only heard of Clavindar and has yet to ever visit. With being the best metal worker, he was always busy. Humans and Rharv's used to come from a far to get things made from him. He doubted if any of the

Arglar, had ever visited. If any had, they concealed themselves well.

He's only heard of them and never actually laid eyes on one. As far as he knew they sounded like a myth, like the Choroac's, the elusive creatures of the two Northern forests, Bristle and Forhown. Said to be a lucky charm if caught.

Maybe Viå was right about going to Clavindar. He hasn't heard about any Arglar being used for slavery around Ulderelm. Perhaps, they were there hiding, staying to the trees.

Not more than a half hour past and the four they were waiting on finally came through the trees. Valcoon was concerned by the fact that Kyö was not his glowing self and the trees were ever so much darker with the haze that shadowed Ulderelm.

"What happened?" He asked, deeply concerned.

"Kyö, did not follow the plan and ended up getting himself into trouble." Viå said, irritated.

"These woods are much darker now, since the darkness." Valcoon stated.

"We'll move along slowly, and I'll take the lead, since I have sensitive ears, unless there's someone here who is capable of getting us to Clavindar much safer?" Viå said.

"We Rharv have poor eyesight in dark places but in the light, we can see for almost miles. I know; a moot point." Valcoon mentioned.

Viå lead them slowly along, opening up her ears, listening very intently for any sign of life but thus far, the forest was as quiet as it has been since they had entered.

They came to a split in the path that went in three directions. She stopped to inspect the trial. Each one was just as worn down as the next.

"Sagfrin, do you know which path to take?" Viå asked.

"So far we've been traveling West and slightly South. I would expect that taking the path to the right would lead us up North. It's been awhile since I've been to Clavindar and these woods are different to me after the years and I've never traveled in the dark, also I can fly, remember?

"I would guess straight, it makes the most sense. It doesn't look like these trails have been used in years." She said.

"Straight it is." Viå said to herself.

Deeper into the forest they went. The sound of water was loud in Viå's ears. There was a river close by. She did her best to drown the sound of passing water out, so she can hear over it, but she was having difficulties doing so.

"I can't hear as well anymore!" She mentioned to Sagfrin.

"Umm, Viå, there seems to be a problem with the passenger." Kyö said.

"What is it?" She asked concerned.

"She is going mad." He said.

Viå approached the side hatch and had Kyö open himself slowly. As soon as it cracked,

Dianna was throwing an arm through, trying to attack them or get free.

"Dianna, what's going on?!" Viå asked mentally. There was no response. "Dianna!" Viå screamed at her.

"I can't stop myself. I'm going to try and hurt you! I don't know why!" She said in an innocent tone and panicked.

"Kyö, open up!" Viå ordered.

Dianna jumped at Viå, scratching, and biting but made no contract. Viå bound her hands up and Dianna continued to bite at her, then proceeded to kick at her.

"Bindings, anyone?!" Viå called forth.

One of the Rharv's immediately brought over some rope and quickly had Dianna immobile. She fought against the bindings, screaming. A Rharv quickly put a cloth into her mouth. She continued to scream in muffled tones.

"Whatever is going on, it can't be good." Sagfrin said, ruffling her chest feathers.

"I'll put her back within Kyö to keep her

quiet. We need to end this nightmare. I hope I'm right and we can find help in Clavindar." Viå said.

They continued on. The water was even louder once they got to it. The bridge over a massive river was looking a bit finished. Viå wasn't too sure if it would hold even her.

The fall to the river was a good drop and the shallowness of it most likely would kill anyone who fell in. She advised that they all cross one at a time to keep any significant weight off of it, just in case.

She called Sagfrin over to have her look at the water. It was a diluted red. Sagfrin shrugged, having no idea as to why.

A young Rharv suggested that Kyö could take them across but Viå said it would take too long and time was one thing that could not wait. The distance of the bridge wasn't that far but it was long enough that if it were to break, there would be no escape from the fall.

Kyö and Sagfrin flew to the other side to wait. Viå went first across the bridge, she figured with her speed and other attributes that if it were to break she could save herself, then they would use Kyö.

She stepped onto the first rung, testing its strength against her weight. She wasn't that heavy in her mind and figured the Rharv's outweighed her by at least thirty plus. She bounced up and down, it proved strong enough.

She visually inspected each rung before she stepped onto it, to avoid a potential break but they all appeared structurally sound and so far, they proved sturdy.

Once across Valcoon followed, a lot slower than Viå. She guessed that he must fear heights. He pushed through whatever made him give pause and successfully crossed.

Vulcil came next, with a much quicker pace, the bridge moved beneath him, but he never hesitated.

All were across but the young Rharv who insisted on riding within Kyö. He stopped short of the bridge, looking around nervously.

Viå wished he would have mentioned that he was frightened of heights.

He stood stiff with panic. Beads of sweat had formed upon his forehead. His long brown mustache blew in the breeze. He looked across at everyone.

"Are you okay?" Viå asked him mentally.

He looked at her. "Just taking in the scenery!" He yelled across. He slowly reached up with his long arms and gripped the rope handrails. With one foot, he placed it on the first rung and froze.

"This is taking too long, I'm going to go get him!" Viå said to no one and told the young Rharv to wait.

She gracefully crossed back across the bridge. "I'm going to carry you." She told him.

"What?! No! I got this!" He said to her.

"We don't have time to wait, you are more than welcome to stay here and wait for our return, except I have no idea how long that may be, or you can cross now!" She said firmly looking into his green eyes.

"Go, I'll follow." He said.

Viå went along with the idea but she was unsure if the bridge could support them both. It creaked beneath their weight. One step at a time they moved. With each step towards the middle, the bridge seemed to take on more stress.

She wondered how long it's been since it was used, judging by the age of the tracks on the paths, a very long time. She paid extra close attention to the ropes as they walked. It looked pretty solid but there was always a potential for it snapping.

Halfway, her confidence in the bridge was good. She had no worries that they would make it across without fail.

Finally, to the other side, her young adult mind let her feelings get the best of her. "Next time, just tell me or us that you need help, we don't have time for mistakes or delays!" She fumed.

He looked at her ashamed. The others looked on with concern. Up to this point, she had a pretty cool head but now she was on edge.

Sagfrin looked at her with different eyes. This was a young woman who was tossed into fixing a world that she was not a part of, so she could understand her mood. Growing up without her mother or her father and with only Kyö to talk to, all those years would be hard. At some point this had to break her mentally. Sagfrin didn't think Viå would ever be a little girl again. This was going to harden her, change her and hopefully not turn her into something else entirely; a nightmare.

Viå remained quiet the rest of the trip, listening intently for any intruders. Her thoughts were placing a heavy weight upon her. She took her breaths in slowly and filtered through her thoughts and removed the ones that were causing her grief.

Out in the distance, Viå could see part of a structure, a house, or a building. She had everyone pause and wait as she went to investigate. It wouldn't matter anyways if they were attacked because there was nowhere to run. They were boxed in and the only way in and out was the path they came in on, as far as she knew.

As she crept out of the trees, she heard no sounds. It was just another dead town but unlike Border it wasn't burned to the ground.

She had never seen anything like it before. The structure on the ground was a home but there were stairs and bridges that lead to homes in the trees. She could only imagine what it would have been like with people and creatures roaming around.

It was a beautiful place. Everything was green but without the sun it was beginning to turn brown. The water in the earth was still trying to give it life.

"So far, it's clear." Viå said to them all touching their minds.

The group came out into the open space, marveling at the scenery. "Wow, this place is amazing! I should have visited back in the day." Valcoon said to himself. "Perhaps if I'm still alive after all this, I'll make my home here." He concluded.

Viå searched the town with her ears, listening for anyone, but heard nothing. "It's bizarre that the Nightmare left this place alone!" Viå said to Sagfrin.

"I honestly never gave thought to the fact that I have not seen any Arglar out in the land, used as slaves. If the Nightmare had not come here, where are they?" She said curiously.

"Arglar? Why have you not mentioned them before?" Viå asked.

"I forgot. They're not the most traveled race. This town was looked over by an elder named Piko, he and a few humans would come and go between trade routes. Where everyone went is a mystery.

"I'm not particularly knowledgeable in their race. Some say they have powers and others say they never age." Sagfrin answered.

"Never age? So, they stay as newborn's?" Viå asked, bewildered.

"I don't know!" Sagfrin admitted.

"We age! Just very slowly" A voice said coming into Viå's mind.

"Who is this, that can speak and listen in to a private conversation of one's mind?" Viå asked, looking around.

"We heard you all the way through the forest. I can say, you're not the quietest group but you're not the loudest either. To answer your question, goddess. I am Deseri." The voice said.

Viå's eyes were wide, how did this woman know she was a goddess?

"Because your thoughts are open and not only that, but I can smell the power running through you." The voice said. "Also, I'm not a woman!" The voice spoke out loud from behind them.

They all turned around and up on the first structure they seen upon entering was a creature that was obviously female and definitely not a woman.

She was beautiful and shaped like a woman. She had on no clothing, she stood exposed and not ashamed. She was covered with tiny dark grey hairs from face to foot. She had long black hair that was tied in knots and draped over one shoulder. She leapt down in front of them and walked very elegantly towards Viå.

Viå had a strange feeling rush through her, that she had never felt before. She could feel her face turn red. She didn't shy away from the female creature, although she wanted to advert her eyes from hers.

They were gold and starry, Viå thought she could see the universe in them. Her lips were non-existent, and her smile showed teeth similar to hers but with longer pointed ones on the bottom.

Her nose was similar down towards the tip but up towards her eyes it widened out into her brow line, which made her eyes further apart. Her ears were strangely different, they came to a point at the top and had two more points that followed down towards the bottom of the ear lobes.

"Why have you come and with an elder?

Their kind abandoned us and Ulderelm years ago. They were supposed to be our protectors from this threat!" Deseri stated harshly, glaring at Sagfrin.

"Would you be willing to listen to reason?" Sagfrin asked her.

"I already know why. I've been reading your minds. It still doesn't justify your actions. Your kind let us down! Left us all to die." She fumed.

"I've come..." Viå started to say but cut herself off, knowing that these creatures knew already.

"If you don't want us to know your thoughts, then shut it off. Think of nothing and then stack that nothing upon your thoughts and keep it in the forefront of your minds. That will shield them." Deseri said, turning towards the Rharv's who were basically drooling over her. "Especially you all!" She added sternly

"I apologize for our thoughts. You can't really blame us though." Valcoon said averting his eyes.

"No, but I and our kind deserve respect and if you can't show us that then I'm afraid we may have problems." She said flatly, pausing on him. She turned towards Viå, looking at her.

"We will join you, only because the facts are, we all are going to die if this threat isn't removed. Also, you seem to be very short in numbers and I believe we can help with that.

"I also know you are doubting yourself. Don't." She said looking deep into Viå's hazel eyes.

"Why is it that you have been spared from slavery?" Viå asked.

"I think it's obvious. The minds of fools are easy to read. When the Molgren's came, we traveled deeper into the forest where none would dare travel. They were going to burn it all down. But the one who leads them, said that they could use it as a source for building, to collect fallen trees.

"They had already began cutting it down in the Northern part. Every day they get closer to here." She said.

"Is it just your kind?" Viå asked.

"No. A few humans are here but some won't be joining us for their age will only hinder our success." She answered.

"Weapons? Will you be needing them?" Valcoon asked, concerned.

"We have them." She said. Still looking at Viå, she told them all to follow and then turned to lead.

They walked through the town and followed to where the trees made a tunnel. Viå could see grave markers. Once they were all out in the open of the grave yard, they noticed that all the graves were full of loose dirt.

"After the shaking of Ulderelm, the dead rose up and started heading North. Their thoughts were their own and they questioned things. A few were thinking of us, the ones who were related and friends but their free will had been tampered with and they could not make another choice. They had to obey the command, to travel North.

"We watched them rise up out of their

graves and leave. The sight was a frightening one. Do you know what's going on?" Deseri asked, already knowing that answer, having read their thoughts.

"As you have already known, we have a dead one with us. A young girl named Dianna. She's under the mind frame of ending us against her free will." Viå stated.

"I do know of her, yes and I'm afraid that she will hinder us but now that you're here we can head North and take out the one's destroying our home and then onward to Drenchin, so that you can end this madness." Deseri stated, still looking deep into Viå's eyes.

Viå was beside herself that this creature could have such strong faith in her. She knew not how this Arglar could know the powers she possessed, when she didn't even know it herself. She was thankful for the confidence coming from a stranger.

"Why have you not taken them out on your own?" Sagfrin asked.

"The numbers those filthy beasts have are

more than we can handle and with the display of courage I witnessed within your minds, we can easily take them all out and free the humans they have enslaved, deserter." Deseri said bitterly, giving Sagfrin another glare.

"I'm sorry for abandoning you all in desperate times. We did what we felt was right and what made sense at the time. If we would have tried to fight, we would have died and then Viå would have come without anyone to guide her!" Sagfrin said, pleading her case.

Deseri ignored her and turned to walk back towards the town. "It's time for us to go." She said.

Suddenly out of the trees came the Arglar. They were many and all female of different shades of brown and grey. All of them were beautiful and carried themselves the same as Deseri.

A brown haired Arglar with long black hair and amber eyes that sparkled like Deseri's approached, holding two spears, glaring at Sagfrin. She handed Deseri a spear and then fell in behind her.

They took a different path out of the town, heading Northeast. Like the other paths this one was not used either. Viå glanced back and saw a few humans had joined them and from the windows, watched the elderly and a couple children. They were waving goodbye.

The Dilemma

The rules were simple. Do not show yourself to your creations. Sure, the created ones believed that there were gods and they would be correct.

The loophole was fairly simple by design. Once a created one was made, the god of that world, placed its own blood within it, linking it to them. Which, through that link could you interact with that created one, since it was a part of you.

Throughout the battles that Rendren and Shalg had, they had infused their blood with a few creations. The ones chosen to be infused were who was appointed the leaders of the world during that time of the game played.

The last time when they had wiped the slate

and began to rebuild, Rendren had done the unthinkable and created the Nightmare.

Instead of infusing his god blood with a creation, he infused himself within the shell of the Nightmare, which gave the Nightmare immortal strength and god like invincibility, but it came with consequences that he was not aware of.

Rendren believed that he would still have the same powers as a god within the Nightmare, but he was mistaken, a lesson learned the hard way and now he was trapped.

Since he was stuck within his own creation without his god powers, he needed a plan. So, he figured that, in order to get out of the Nightmare, he needed to win this game but his brother Shalg had countered him again. He thought that he could win being who he was but that was proven wrong.

When they laid out the platform for their new game he had the upper hand. He gathered up his forces of Molgren's and waged war upon Ulderelm. He underestimated the elders, who called forth his brother and he in turn created Thondrous.

Thondrous was all power and heavy hitting. Each punch hurt, like a mountain falling on top of you. Thondrous felt no pain, which was the reason for his victory. The Nightmare tried everything to stop him, even the scepter of tribulation had no effect.

The Nightmare raised mountains and dropped them on Thondrous but Thondrous burst through. He was unstoppable for not being a god.

Blow after blow the Nightmare and Thondrous returned. Both were equal. Rendren realized that Shalg was the better god and after the game was played, he would tell him so.

Events fell in place that set the game on pause. The elders had found a way to best the Nightmare. They used the light of the sun and enchanted Thondrous with light. It was the Nightmare's weakness, which Rendren had failed to counter.

It was a flaw in character design that Rendren over looked. He wanted the Nightmare to be able to use dark power to bring chaos to Shalg's forces but forgot the balance that was needed and then he was trapped and placed within Moudrous mine.

Within, his powers were weak. When he found the elemental blood pixies. He was surprised for they were from a previous game and were his brother's creations and yet they somehow survived when he and Shalg remade this one. He wasn't going divulge the Shadow of this information, in case it would forfeit his god powers, although they cist to work within the Nightmare's shell but he didn't want to take a chance and put Shalg into limbo.

When the darkness came; that did weaken the defenses in place to keep him confined. He knew where the keys were located, since he was a god he could scurry the land with his mind, which was how he was able to locate the Shadow but now that the darkness has increased, it has given him more dark powers but has taken away most of his god abilities, making him the Nightmare.

His god blood still worked to tie bonds but that was it. Since his powers had shifted from a god to the Nightmare's dark powers, his thirst to drink blood had increased and his need to fuck was also more sporadic. It has now become him.

He tried to scurry the land several times but got nowhere. He was becoming more and more of this beast that he created. He wanted to contact his brother and give him the victory he deserved and seek help in getting out of the Nightmare but now trapped in the shell and with the dark haze, he could not look into the other side.

He was sure when the blood pixies had told him of the darkness, his brother would have consulted with the sole creator, to seek information and Shalg had to have wondered where he was during that meeting.

Now, his only hope was to finish this game and hope his brother could help him get free.

The elders blood had his brothers blood in them and if he drank it, he could get back his powers. It was wishful thinking.

As he had another woman mount him, his thoughts were on this new threat that had taken out an encampment by themselves, along with an elder and freed his metal workers. If he could scurry the land he could find this threat and take them out but now he would have to wait until one of his informants brought word to him and hopefully soon.

He finished fornicating and since she didn't conceive he took a bite into her neck and began sucking the warm, sweet blood out of her body. Her eyes rolled back, and a moan escaped her lips. He pulled harder, frustrated by his dilemma, and then snapped her neck and tossed her across the room. Her body tumbled across the floor.

"Fuck!" He yelled. He screamed out in anger. He couldn't wait, he'll go get his answers and get them now. He knocked down the doors and broke through the hall wall. He took to the sky. This world was his. This game, he was going to win. His god status reinstated. He was waiting no more.

Elkron And Shug

Without his cock attached to himself, he was feeling less of a male than normal. That damn Rharv took his manhood. Feeling pissed and ultimately depressed about his genital being bitten off. The other Molgren's had started in on him.

He hacked a few of his beasts for their banter, to let them know he was still in charge with or without his cock. They immediately shut their mouths and averted their eyes whenever he came around.

He couldn't believe she had come back to life, how the other dead had come back. "What the fuck was going on?!" Was his retort.

He sat on the edge of a table with some strong drink. His cock sat next to him in a bowl. He looked at it, missing it. The dirty, bloody rags pressed against his groin had slowed the bleeding but anytime he got agitated, it would start bleeding again.

Not feeling confident about anyone else, he decided to try to put it back on himself. He had some string and a needle. He poured some of the drink into the bowl and then removed the rags and poured it onto his nub. It burned like crazy.

He shoved the needle into the skin. It stretched as he pushed, forcing it through. It made a popping sound as it broke through the skin. "Fuck! Shit! Ahhhh!" He yelled.

Grabbing his cock out of the bowl and shaking the drink off, he poked the needle through it and then slide it down the thread until the two halves touched. Being overwhelmed with everything, he had forgot to make sure it was lined up correctly. Since it wasn't, he had to start over, sticking the needle through the right area of his unattached cock.

He screamed throughout the whole process

until he had successfully stitched it back on. Whether it will work again, was going to be the actual success. He stood up looking down at his work. It hurt but overall it looked ok to him. He poured more of the strong drink on his cock, wincing with the pain.

He wrapped it up in a somewhat cleaner rag and put on some leggings that he had found. He walked around the room slowly, seeing how it felt. Not good, but at least the damn thing was attached again.

He exited the room and rounded up his beasts. He ordered them onward towards the East. He had an obligation, to burn everything and leave nothing standing. Like old times. He was going to find these fucking elders and they were going to bring him peace of mind for his cock.

He could blame the Nightmare, but it was really the elders who had pulled him from retirement. He was excited obviously about his mission but now he wanted to get it over with.

Now with a few hundred humans on their side, which were fed and had gotten some much needed rest. They had themselves a decent size force. The humans took advantage of the nearby stream to bath and many of them started to workout, doing push-ups and sit-ups and working with their rye cutting blades, swinging them around as weapons. They were feeling like themselves again.

Elkron and Sirium had decided to head South towards the brick makers, since it was very close to the burned down town of Quezen. The only thing left standing was a building that housed the Molgren's, while they looked over the rye fields. Elkron suggested they stay there and let the slaves get some more rest.

The following day, Elkron suggested they carry on but the humans insisted that they take this time to cope with being free. He was sympathetic to their want since most of these humans had been in slavery since they were just children.

Their backs and bodies were marked up

from being whipped with whatever objects the ones who punished them could find. A little while longer couldn't hurt, but at the same time, it could.

So, he gave in and spent his time consulting with the elders and Sirium, figuring out their plan. At some point, Elkron hoped to find Sagfrin. He missed her company and hoped that she was still doing okay and above all, still alive.

He looked at the warrior Shring as they were sparring with each other. They were never not, even as they marched, practicing tactics. He couldn't believe that these creatures were from a world before. He couldn't imagine going into a place and then coming back out and then everything you knew was gone, changed. The fear of that must have been overwhelming.

As the forces were getting ready to sleep, the world around them shook violently. Elkron and the other elders jumped in the air. Down below everything was shaking and then it stopped. Elkron landed and rushed inside the building, checking to see if they were all okay.

"What was that?!" Tyhim asked.

Elkron shrugged. He has read and heard tales of earth trembling's before but never witnessed one and it would appear that neither have the Shring. They all waited for another rumble, but it never came. So, they all rested, getting ready for what they will soon face.

They marched South in open land, knowing full well that they would be spotted. Elkron had no worries at this point. The Shring held their own well, so taking these ones out would not be an issue, unless the elemental sprites were around waiting for them. That fear was in him since he was caught.

He knew the Shadow would have raced back to the Nightmare with news about what happened; that most likely would have not been good for him.

Out in the distance a loud sound came. It sounded like a horn and was most likely an alarm. Any moment the very fast and very deadly horde of Molgren's would be a blur, rushing at them.

As he had predicted, they were coming. A blur in the distance, he quickly scribbled in the dirt. "Get ready!" But needlessly he didn't need to write anything, for their blades were out awaiting the advancing horde.

They came in fast; the four elders and the Shring stood still. The four elders were going to use the earth to cause a wave of destruction. They stepped out front, timing their power, waiting on the right moment to release it.

The Molgren's were closer, closer. The elders placed the tips of their wings to the ground and pushed power into it, then pulled up. The tips of their wings to the sky. The first wave came. They alternated to the other side, sending a second rumbling wave.

The speed of the Molgren's was no match for the mountains of dirt and rock waves crashing down upon them and throwing them backwards.

The elders flew into the air and began to

throw air wisps, stirring up dust. The Shring rushed into the dust and started to take out the Molgren's, one, two, three, at a time.

Once the dust settled, not one Molgren was left standing. Elkron almost felt invincible, with the force they had. They were almost untouchable, but this was just the beginning and had a much greater battle ahead.

When they arrived at their destination, they killed the last of the Molgren's and freed the slaves, which were mostly naked women, covered in mud. They were so happy to be free that they began hugging all of them and then raced off towards the lake to wash the mud off.

After, they all stood naked, except for the dozen or so men.

"Why are you naked?" Sirium asked the women.

A blonde stepped forward. "We used to be a part of the Nightmare's fuck circle. When we were in the city, up in the main chamber, we were intoxicated by the Nightmare, ever so burning with passion to be fucked by him. All of us waited our turn.

"We are the ones who conceived his offspring and once we were pregnant, we were taken to a part of the tower to give birth. Once doing so, the Nightmare was finished with us and sent us out into Ulderelm to work as slaves.

"We all want our lives back. Those Molgren's raped all of us every night and sometimes during the day. We are glad that they no longer walk the land and for that we are in your debt." She said.

"Will you all fight with us?! Harphrum asked. Revealing herself as a female, maybe to persuade them that even though they are women they could still fight.

The men were more than willing. The women paused, hesitant. "How can we fight?" The blonde asked.

"With vengeance. Use the hurt and anger you feel inside. You said you want your lives back and to do that, you must take it back!

You offered your debt to us and we ask that you join us in the fight to bring peace to Ulderelm!" Harphrum said determined to persuade these women.

They looked at each other and a red head stepped forward. "I will fight! I want these beasts dead!" She said.

"As will I!" Another said. Soon all the women had joined them.

"Good. Now we need weapons and clothes!" Harphrum mentioned.

"We're good without clothing. We've been nude, almost our whole lives and so it bothers us not!" A brunette confirmed. If any other woman felt the need to be clothed, they stayed quiet about it.

Westward was their next plan and Elkron was having doubts about this war. Although they had a good number, it was still far from being enough. He knew the Nightmare had multitudes. Around twenty to one. He knew to, that if the Nightmare and the Shadow were joining together in the final battle, they were doomed.

He certainly hoped that the savior had shown up. That shooting star could have been just that and he could be leading all these people and creatures to their deaths. He looked out into the distance and stared at Mount Fire and thought about Sagfrin and hoped she had found the savior.

Shug lead his forces down around Drenchin, into the wide-open space of the dry lands. The town border was to the South, but he burned that place down years ago. He decided to head East towards Lantro lake. Next, they would head South into the mountains. Out in the distance he could see a mass number of figures approaching and did not know if it was his own or the enemy.

He was hopeful that it was his enemies, so that he could take out his aggression on them.

As they got closer, he noticed the elders soaring above the throng. This was them. He ordered his squad to flank left and right, surrounding the force coming their way.

He was going to make them all pay. They were going to eat them all! He was going to enjoy this.

The two forces met head on. Heads came off shoulders, bodies split in two, blood sprayed, and guts fell. It was a sight to behold. Shug was bewildered that it was his own forces that were being ran through, since his race was the most feared and strongest.

The hooded figures were fast and the weapons they carried were a threat to his Molgren's. He noticed, just a stab and they were turning to dust, shortly after.

The elders were using the ground and air to do their damage. He was furious. He put his shield in front with his meaty arm bracing it. His dagger firmly gripped. The elder was faced away. This was going to be too easy.

He stabbed at the elder, but the dagger did not come near. It had somehow deflected. The elder turned towards him coming in contact with his shield. Shug swung the shield at the elder, knocking it backwards, sending it tumbling across the earth.

Elkron shook himself from the blow the Molgren had just landed on him with his shield, which got rid of his own shield. The Molgren was large. Elkron tried to summon an air wisp but wasn't fast enough. The Molgren kicked him in his feathery side, which sent him rolling in the dirt.

Elkron got up and leaped at the beast, feet first but it just grabbed him and slammed him to the ground. It climbed on top of him and began smashing his face into the dirt; over and over.

"Fuck you, you stupid piece of shit! It's all your fault! You and your kind are going to pay!" The Molgren screamed at him as it continued to whack his face into the ground.

Suddenly the weight lifted and

Elkron heard struggling from behind. He turned and through his own blood he could see Sirium was there with a light dagger at the

Molgren's throat.

Elkron motioned for Sirium to release him. Sirium didn't question, nor try to argue. The Molgren rose to his full height, roughly eight foot tall. Almost twice of Elkron.

Shug stared down upon this feathered creature. It's face all fucked up. A smiled curled on Shug's lip and faded just as quickly as it came. Around him was nothing but three other feathered freaks and the hooded figures. He was finished, he had no else. His horde was gone.

Even once he killed this puny fuck, the rest would destroy him but right now he didn't care. He tossed the shield aside and then his knife.

His cock was in pain from his blood pumping, with all the excitement. Looking down at his leggings he noticed they were covered in his cock blood. He didn't give a fuck anymore.

He turned his attention back on the creepy

elder, who walked over and kicked the knife back. Shug turned his head to the side in confusion.

Normally it was custom to go head on and try to murder one another with just their own strengths, no weapons, or tricks.

This elder wanted to die quickly, without a fight. Pity, he thought. He was hoping to find out how strong this ugly fuck was but who was he to argue.

Shug picked up his own knife and readied himself. Elkron stood ready as well. The two creatures of Ulderelm, both birthed into this timeline, faced one another.

Shring gathered around, from the past, a different time but here now. They looked on from beneath their hoods with anticipation. All of them raised their glowing dagger's high in the air and kept them there.

Elkron looked at the ugly Molgren. Shug looked at the ugly elder. Shug rushed in, in a blur swinging the blade. Elkron could hardly see him. He jumped back but the Molgren was too fast and shoved his dagger into Elkron's breast.

Shug stood with wide evil red eyes and his yellow teeth barred, pushing the knife harder into Elkron. Sirium tossed his glowing dagger towards Elkron, who caught it with his foot. The blade was backwards. He dropped it. The pain from the knife in him was growing.

Shug looked down at the other dagger and picked it up and then went to shove it inside Elkron as well, but the glowing dagger would not penetrate. Shug looked at the blade in confusion and then his hand turned black and burst into powder, floating away with the wind, dropping the blade. Then the blackness trailed up his arm and consumed the rest of him, turning him to ash. His whole body followed his hand towards the East with the wind.

Elkron fell to the ground, blood pooling in the dirt. His chest feathers coated in his thick blood. A healer rushed over and yanked the knife free. Blood squirted from the large open wound and started pooling on his chest. She quickly laid her hands on him. Instantly the wound was no more.

He was light headed from the amount of blood loss, but he made the effort to scribble in his blood. "Thank you so much!"

She nodded and raced off to help her fellow Shring. Not too many were injured, so the healers didn't have their hands very full.

Sirium knelt down beside Elkron. "You did good, you were definitely dead in that match, but stupidity won. It seems the power in these dagger's, thanks to you and your friends are what is going to help us win this battle." He stated.

Elkron smiled. "Shall we continue on?!" Elkron wrote.

"Let's!" Sirium said.

A Joyous Reunion

The fight with the timber crew was too easy. The Molgren's had their axes and knives and were quick but they were no match for their group. The humans doing all the tree fall were more than thankful to be free.

These slaves were fit but exhausted and under fed. They were more than willing to join in the up rise, to bring peace to Ulderelm. These men who have not seen a woman in a really long time kept ogling at Viå and the Arglar.

Though they were not human, did not mean that they were not a pretty sight and given their confidence and lack of clothing made them even more appealing.

Viå admired the Arglar, with their graceful

fighting skills. They were so delicate in every move executed, it was as if they weren't even trying. They were not near as fast as she or the Molgren's and not as strong as the Rharv's, but they were very agile and that proved just as deadly.

The Rharv's were quick to praise their amazing skills and were thankful they were on the same side.

Deseri made it clear to the humans about their graphic thoughts and told them to keep them tightly locked up. She warned them that most of the Arglar would easily gut them if they felt threatened by a vulgar thought.

They nodded their understanding with wide fearful eyes, then like the Rharv's, averted their attention elsewhere. Deseri smiled playfully at Viå.

Being North of the Clavin forest put them just South of the fires running from Mount Fire. It was the single highest mountain apart from the ones further up North, but it was massive. They were now in what used to be and maybe still is, Molgren territory.

Sagfrin assured them that most went inland to Drenchin and have made it their home. Drenchin was massive, so invading it was going to be a chore. The only positive thing about Drenchin was that Sagfrin knew every inch of it but then again, that was years ago and chances of it being the same as she remembers were very slim.

Traveling through the land of Mount Fire was hot. As Sagfrin had stated, the land was actually free of Molgren's. It was now just a place of danger if you were not careful. The only thing now was to head North to this other encampment. The dead that have risen had supposedly gone this way as well.

Viå and Kyö had to escape a planet of dead before and so this was nothing new, but this was a different world. She didn't know what or why the dead had risen and if she had to guess, she would guess that the dead were probably headed to Drenchin and when she asked Sagfrin of her thoughts. She said that was possible, but nothing was for sure.

They have traveled most of the Southern parts of Ulderelm and had a significantly strong group of allies but if the dead were on the nightmare's side and if there was still a mass amount of Molgren's in Drenchin, would their strength and abilities be enough?

She wished that she could just head to Drenchin and fight the Nightmare but without knowing his strengths and weaknesses, she could easily die and then everything would die, and she would not be a hero and she would be a failure.

The creator said she had the potential to end the purple Haze, the darkness that was polluting the universe, but she needed help, if she was going to win and she was thankful for the help she did have.

She looked at her companion and was saddened by his light gone. He was her best friend, they've been together for a long time and losing him would be the death of her. Even though he was technically not a living thing, he was to her.

Coming around the fire pits and beginning to head true North, they spotted figures out in the distance coming from the East. They were too far away to notice anything particular. Could it be the dead or another horde of Molgren's? Could this be a massive force that was the end of this war, Viå wasn't sure.

Sagfrin and Deseri wanted to hide and wait, to see what this throng of dark figures out on the horizon were. If it was a small batch of Molgren's then they could take them out. The more of the dark creatures they killed the less there would be in the end.

If this group ended up being a massive force, that was impossible to overtake, then they would retreat back towards the Clavin forest and figure out their next move.

At some point, regardless of numbers they were going to have to dive into the throng and fight. It was Viå's destiny. It was why she was here. She could not let her mother down or her uncle's and definitely not her father. She needed some time to think, to give her mind clarity.

She went to Kyö and touched her friend. "I love you, Kyö." She put her face on him. He was no longer warm.

"I love you as well. What is wrong?" He asked.

"I'm feeling overwhelmed right now. Our numbers are few and time is short, and it does not appear that there are any more forces to join us. Even with heading North to the next location, which would only give us a few hundred more, maybe." She said, closing her eyes.

"That may be but from what I have witnessed, the skills that these races have are more powerful than any amount of Molgren's or anything we have witnessed so far and would lead us to a victory. Not to mention they have you." He said, comforting.

"We do have the skills, that is for sure, but a hundred to one just doesn't seem fair. We can't go on waiting any longer. The longer we wait the more time the darkness has to grow stronger." She stated, rubbing her face on him.

"Viå, I believe everything will be okay. You are the one the creator chose, as am I the one he chose as well, and I would think that he wouldn't have left it up to us to save the universe if he didn't believe we could do it!" He said in a rather stern tone.

Viå took a long deep breath, releasing it and turned, leaning her back on him, getting the comfort she was needing. "You're right about that. I can't wait until we are finished, and we can go home."

"I know, soon that time will come. You need to put that in the back of your mind and focus on what we have come here to do." He said.

"Thanks, my friend. I love you and when this is finished I promise we'll get you fixed." She said confidently.

"I'm missing my glow already." He mentioned.

Viå laughed and then gave him a kiss.

"Thanks for the talk!"

"I'm always here."

He was right. She needed to focus on what she needed to do. It was now time. Time to march through Drenchin and kill everyone, bring peace, and bring the universe back in balance. She was now convicted to her cause, more than ever. Her mind was again set straight. To those of Ulderelm and to the universe, she was going to save it all.

Sirium marched out front, followed closely by Elkron in the sky. It was time to go against the Nightmare and his forces and the next stop was around Drenchin, to the North. Time was of the essence and he was more than surprised that they have not yet run into the elemental sprites yet. As dedicated as they were with capturing him and the other elders. It was as if they had just vanished into thin air.

After they saved the slaves and fought the last battle, it was time to get to the metal workers sight but when they arrived it was void of life. Outside the compound, there was so much blood that stained the ground. It was days old, but it proved that something or someone was here, on their side. Perhaps Sagfrin and the savior. Searching around he found a set of tracks that were definitely Sagfrin's, along with some very bizarre ones, which made Elkron pretty excited.

The slaves were gone; free from their shackles. How they removed them was a mystery he hoped to someday find out, since as far as he knows, was the only one that had these Shring with light daggers.

Out in the distance, Mount Fire was getting larger with each step. They avoided Drenchin by crossing down further South. They had one destination in mind and it was not Drenchin, not yet.

They walked, the elders flew. Turning North, something started flying towards them. Sirium halted the troops. Elkron landed beside him and scribbled in the dirt.

Excited, Sagfrin began to take off. Viå was beside herself. "What is it?" She demanded speaking to her mind.

"It's Elkron!" Sagfrin said very excited and flew off without another word. Out in the distance she watched a hooded figure halt the mass of beings. Then another Cremhen landed beside the one who halted the mass. Sanding beat her wings as fast as she could.

Sagfrin glided down towards them and landed, stirring up dust. She now knew in her heart that she loved Elkron and that she couldn't live without him. In the dirt was the words: "It's Sagfrin, an ally." When she landed, she saw no one else, just Elkron. She wrapped him in her wings and he the same. They kissed, passionately. She looked into his eyes. He smiled at her and she returned the same.

There was a lot of catching up to do and no time to do it, but they made the time, for it needed to be said, because they had to catch each other up with everything that has taken place.

Trial and Error

The Nightmare who was Rendren flew, pissed off at the fate of his rule and his predicament of being trapped in this shell of a body with no way, except possibly the elders to get back to his brother, so Shalg could help him.

Out in the city below the Molgren's and now the dead were thick. His enemies had no chance in prevailing against him. He had this war. He had not heard word from his blood pixies and by now they should have been back. He did notice Shug's destruction to the North and he grimaced at the sight.

He knew not where to go, he was flying blind. He needed answers and was not going to wait until it knocked on his door. Out towards the West, the fire was oozing down Mount Fire. He should have made that his home, built a palace and held up there. It would have made the perfect defense against his brothers forces before his imprisonment.

Next time they play, he most certainly will consider creating an impenetrable fortress, making it full of death traps. He knew not but his wondering mind was taking him towards Mount Fire.

In the distance there was a throng of figures about a quarter of the size of his force. Could it be Shug or another squad of his or, it could very well be his enemies and his slaves. One way to know for sure. He thrust his massive black wings and headed in that direction.

Everyone was in good spirit, having increased their force and having the most skilled warriors of all Ulderelm, with a few hundred humans, but they could hold their own, even with their limited abilities.

Viå was feeling a little better now about

their group and after her talk with Kyö, she was feeling confident again. She was glad to see Sagfrin's friends were doing great and she was intrigued by the story Elkron had told about Moudrous mine and the glowing daggers and about the Shring being from another world apart from this one. It seemed very unreal, but she knew about gods and their ways. Her mother's own story was like a fable, but she was here, a quarter god, so she believed anything was possible.

"Fuck! Something is headed this way and it's huge!" A man shouted. The whole mass stopped and turned around and sure enough, a large black mass was flying towards them.

"It's the Nightmare!" Elkron said to Viå.

This was it, out here with no horde to help him. He was large and black. His size was intimidating. As he got closer, she could see how ugly this beast was, with large blood red eyes and sharp burgundy nails and complete naked. In his large black hand was the scepter of tribulation.

He flew past overhead. Viå turned towards the group and grabbed Deseri by her shoulders. "Get everyone to run back towards the South. I am going to go out a head, to lead him away and I don't want anyone getting killed. If his scepter is as powerful as they say it is, then he could easily end all of us now! Now go!" She ordered.

This was it, to see what she was up against. To learn his strengths and his weakness, if he had any. She pulled her swords free from their home and took off in a blur.

The Nightmare spun back around. She called out to him with her swords ready, her uncle's swords.

He watched the mass take off as one single woman ran the opposite direction, pulling swords free. Was this the one to stop him? A woman? He wasn't just going to kill this woman, he was going to fuck her and suck her life out of her body first, conception or not! A women's voice entered his mind. "Come and face me!" It was the single woman.

He landed, leaving deep divots in the dirt. Dust rolled up beneath his large feet. The large nails of his toes dug into the ground as he walked. He approached her. She was beautiful and very young, almost a child. He was really going to enjoy himself. He stopped several yards away from her in case she was more dangerous than she appeared.

"So, you're the one that has come to stop me? You have really caused some stir up with my dark ones." He said in a deep growly voice.

"Your time of rule is over, you will not be a threat no more!" The women said convicted.

He smiled, then chuckled. "Wow! You truly fucking believe your pieces of metal can harm me? You have speed but guess what? So, do I! What else do you fucking have that I don't?!" He growled.

She looked upon his ugly face as he sneered. She could see her allies far off in the South, looking on. She blew her hair off her face. "I'm deadlier than I look, and I'll prove it!"

She shouted.

Wanting to get this over with, she had forgotten her mother's words and they were the most single important ones in combat. "Never make the first move when you're facing off on a single opponent." She rushed in low and to the left, both swords horizontal, left over right.

He simply reached out and grabbed her hair. The momentum jerked her head back hard. He held her up, looking at her pathetically.

He started punching at her with his free hand, but she blocked every heavy swing. Each blow hurt upon impact, but she blocked it out. He lifted her high into the air over his head, her hair was all he had. As she began to flip upside-down, she quickly swung a sword up, cutting her hair off at his knuckles. She felt her blades contact them.

She flew backwards parallel with the ground. She flipped herself over and landed like an animal on all fours. Glancing at his knuckles, he had not one open wound. He was right about her blades not hurting him.

She wasn't going to give up on them yet. He blew the hairs off of his open palm and then waved the scepter at her and lifted her up into the air and held her there and then he simply bright the scepter down, slamming her into the ground, making an impression. Then waved the scepter again, tossing her away. She tumbled across the dirt.

She was going to feel that later. She quickly got up and as he was swinging the rod, she quickly evaded it by rolling and jumping. She did not know how this scepter worked. Was there a line of sight to it or was it a thought? She now knew that she had to keep moving.

She felt the ground rumble behind her, as the Nightmare tried to snag her again with the scepter. This was not going well. She needed to get closer and get around him, but how?

She was going to need to use her strength against his. It would be blow for blow. Ultimately, she needed to get the scepter away from him. She really wished she knew how to use her power.

"Fuck it!" She said under her breath and rushed straight into him with all her speed, ramming him with her shoulder. It knocked him backwards. She stabbed her swords into the ground and began punching his body and he returned his own series of punches.

His fists hurt every time she couldn't block. She wondered if he felt any pain at all when she landed a punch or a kick. He grabbed her by the neck and began to pick her up, but she gripped his wrist and twisted it outward releasing his hand from her throat, then she jump-kicked him in the side of his head. Knocking him to the ground.

He grabbed her ankle before she had time to move and released the scepter to grab her other ankle. He pulled her feet out from under her as he stood at full height. Then he started slamming her into the ground. She did her best to try and put her hands down to stop herself, but the force was too strong.

He repeated the process. Her face smashed

the ground, her chest smashed the ground. She felt her bones break. Dirt was stuck to the blood covering her face. One final ground slam and then he let her go.

She couldn't move from the pain. The Nightmare grabbed the back of her clothing and ripped them off of her.

His genital came to life, from the excitement. He threw her clothes down. Drool fell from his mouth. He put his weight on top of her.

She grunted from beneath him. Her breath was already gone. She had tears in her eyes, her face throbbed, she was a mess. She could feel her legs being forced open. She fought so hard to squeeze them closed but she was too weak from being slammed into the earth. She struggled and cried as she waited for him to do what he was going to do to her. She finally had given up, lost her fight, her valor. The pain she felt, and the hopelessness of her current situation left her in distress, she shut her mind down.

This was not how it was supposed to be. She was in over her head. How was she going to beat this fuck, that was about to do unthinkable things to her?

Suddenly, the weight lifted, and she heard Deseri's voice. "Leave her alone, you, sick fuck!"

"You stupid fucking fools! This is my world!" The Nightmare's voice boomed in Viå's ears.

Viå, sorely and slowly pushed herself up off the ground. The air blew across her naked, bruised and opened wounded body. She could only see out of one eye. She slowly limped along. On the ground at her feet was the scepter of tribulation.

The Nightmare was foolish enough to think, she wouldn't have been helped? That these creatures were afraid of him? They were not afraid; not anymore. Now, he had made a mistake, a mistake that would most likely cost him his life.

She bent down and scooped the scepter up.

It was heavier than it looked. She walked towards her group of allies who were fighting the Nightmare and they were losing bad. Three Arglar were in pieces on the ground. One was the one, that had handed Deseri her weapon back in Clavindar.

Viå lifted the rod and pointed it at the Nightmare and flicked her bruised wrist. The ground erupted beneath him and pushed him up. He flapped a giant wing, balancing himself. He looked at her. His blood eyes, glared at her. His teeth clenched.

She turned her wrist again and slammed him into the ground and then swung her arm out to the side. He used his nails on both hands and feet to keep from being tossed. She dropped the tip of the scepter down, holding him to the ground. All of the creatures rushed in and started to punch, kick and beat the Nightmare with their weapons.

None of weapons did any damage to his thick black flesh. Until he was hit with one of the glowing daggers of the Shring. The

Nightmare roared and broke free and flew up into the air with Sirium by the neck. It was him who had cut the Nightmare. In the air the Nightmare grabbed Sirium's hand, holding the dagger and with his massive black hand ripped off Sirium's arm and then using it, shoved Sirium's dagger into Sirium's own chest.

The Nightmare then bit into Sirium and started sucking out his blood. Viå quickly tried to point the scepter at the beast but it didn't work. He must have been too far away. Next the Nightmare dropped Sirium. He fell into a crumbling heap on the ground.

The Shring rushed in to get to him. Up in the sky, the Nightmare was bleeding badly. The dagger had actually cut him open. It was a sign of hope. Elkron had mentioned that when cut or stabbed by the dagger it made those who are creatures of dark turn to ash. Viå wondered if the Nightmare was going to burst into dust and blow away any second. Of course, he wouldn't, it was never that simple, was it?

The Nightmare seeing that he was wounded and without the scepter flew off, back towards Drenchin. He screamed a high shriek then shouted back. "You are all going to fucking suffer. I'll be waiting. My dark ones are going to murder every last one of you and then they'll eat the meat clean from your bones!"

Viå fell over from the pain and exhaustion. Sagfrin caught her just before she hit the ground and gently laid her down.

The healers were busy with Sirium at the moment, trying to see if they could save him but that was impossible. He was dead, the blood taken from his body was why they could not save him.

A healer came over and laid hands on Viå. She was completely healed within moments. These creatures were amazing and Viå could not be any more grateful to them. The idea of healing yourself or someone instantly was most amazing. Viå could only dream of such powers.

The Shring were completely disheartened and distraught by the loss of their leader, Sirium. They were very upset to the fact that they could not place him among their other leaders within their home, but they had dedicated themselves to this mission and they were now dedicating it to Sirium.

Once this was over they would have to select a new leader but now they all said words over his grave.

The dead Arglar were buried as well. Deseri looked miserable but shared nothing. The Arglar stood quietly over the graves of their own. No tears were shed for their fallen. Viå figured it was their custom.

Viå thought on it and consulted with Sagfrin and then met with Valcoon about acquiring swords made from the glowing metal. He had no idea where to get it but Viå told him what Elkron had said about Moudrous mine. He said that he could make her the most beautiful swords she would ever see. She said she didn't care what they looked like as long as they will hold up against the Nightmare.

Sagfrin wondered if they should even head to the last encampment or if they should head straight for Moudrous mine. Elkron suggested that they could use the last of the slaves in this fight for peace. He said, "What if those last slaves were the fine line between victory or defeat?" Which did make sense.

So, they all headed North to free the last known slaves and to potentially use them to have better odds for a chance at victory.

Swords, Arglar, And the Scepter

After they freed the slaves from the encampment, they headed to Moudrous mine. It was a very long journey and all of their supplies were running dangerously low. They packed what they could get from the encampment, which was not enough to supply them all. They rationed what they could on their journey Southeast.

Viå suggested that they split up, so they could get everyone to the metal workers site and reenergize. She entrusted Elkron with the scepter of tribulation, to keep it safe.

Her, Sagfrin and Kyö could get to the mine and meet them back at the metal worker site. Elkron was hesitant about it, for fear of losing Sagfrin again by another attack from the

Nightmare but Sagfrin insured him that he had nothing to worry about, since any threat would be at Drenchin by now.

Dianna who was bound up within Kyö and sure enough, she was dead brought back. The poor thing. Viå was sad of this little girl's life and was doing what she thought best. She was only trying to kill them because her mind was being forced. None of them had any ideas of what to do with her. Deseri suggested that they end her suffering but that seemed a bit extreme, but she argued the point that she was already dead.

How would you kill something already dead? How? Deseri did have a point. Dianna was at this point, baggage. She wouldn't stop trying to kill them until they were dead and so they could not let her go.

Viå decided to try her powers. She placed her hand on Dianna's head. The little girl was still trying to get at her. She squirmed around trying her best to break free.

Viå closed her eyes and felt the girl. Just

like the shackles, she had darkness coursing through her. A strange darkness that was unlike the powers within the manacles. This darkness flowed in her blood, through her. She couldn't go into the girl, same as the collars, but she was able to dissect her, look at everything in pieces.

How could she extract the darkness from her blood? Could it be as simple as replacing it with happiness as she did with the collars? Dianna would go back to her eternal rest if Viå was successful.

Viå focused on the darkness and again she thought of her mother and her uncles, but it wasn't working this time. Dianna furiously thrashed around. Viå stepped away helpless, at a loss. She needed to help this girl and Ulderelm. So much weighed on her.

She cleared her mind from distracting thoughts and only focused on pure calming moments in her mind. She remembered the flowers of Buriece and the butterflies. She felt her mother's kiss and her warm embracing hugs. She saw her uncle's smiles.

The blue birthmark on her wrist ignited, turning an aqua-green. She was turning her happy moments into power. She felt her connection with her birthmark. She latched on and forced it out of herself and into Dianna. The darkness tried to take over but the purity of Viå's thoughts, overpowered it. The darkness went limp and started to break away. Soon the darkness flowing within Dianna was replaced with peace, emptiness.

Viå felt the blood in Dianna return to its dead self. Dianna went still. Viå opened her eyes with tears in them. She scooped the poor innocent girl up into her arms and handed her off to Valcoon. "Bury her proper, please. She didn't ask for any of this." She said and kissed Dianna's forehead.

Valcoon nodded. "Travel safe." He said and walked away.

Viå climbed inside of Kyö and they took off with Sagfrin at Kyö's side.

It took no time at all to reach Moudrous mine. It was just a crater in the ground, a massive one. On the surface was the glowing Greenite.

Viå jumped out of Kyö and looked around at the ground. Sagfrin landed beside her. "Do you suppose we gather little pieces or one large piece?" Viå asked, wondering which the best option was.

"One large piece, considering if we can transport it. It would probably be most efficient. I'm not sure how well this stuff breaks down. I've only seen it in its weapons and armor form and it was also not in this glowing state." Sagfrin said.

Looking around and picturing the length of her swords, started comparing the glowing Greenite. Once she found a nice large chunk, she drew a sword out and held it beside it. "This should be enough, right?" She asked.

"I would believe so." Sagfrin said.

Kyö inspected the Greenite. "With the density of your swords and the weight of the

Greenite, it should be plenty. Pick the piece up if you can and that should indicate the proper mass for the weight needed." He said.

Viå knelt down and put her fingers under the rock and pulled, lifting it out of the ground. It was much larger than she had anticipated and much more than she needed. "This would do, if others wanted to craft new weapons as well but Kyö would have to transport it and I would need to run." Viå stated.

"The only problem is, our supplies are low, and you need the strength to make that journey on foot." Sagfrin pointed out.

"I can make it. Plus, I can stretch my rations a little further if I need to." She said.

"I'll trust your decision, if you believe it can be done." Sagfrin said with worry on her face.

"Let us go then." Viå confirmed.

Valcoon and Harphrum sat upon the roof of the metal workers site, looking out over the land. The bodies of Molgren's that were once littered across the ground were no longer there, they had like that little girl Dianna, risen from the dead.

Valcoon had buried her respectfully. He laid her body gently down and then with his own hands dug a deep hole and then eased her in and covered her. He thought it best to say a few words. "Uhm, I'm sorry that you had to endure the frightening chaos that happened so long ago. I wish you could have had the life, you were supposed to have. I am glad that Viå was able to put you back to rest and I also hope this grave, suits you. Rest easy Dianna, I will think of you for the rest of my life. Goodbye." His voice chattering the last syllable.

Harphrum and Valcoon had grown close in the few days together since the reunion of the elders. They would consider each other friends and nothing more. The thought of being with one that looked as Harphrum, was not attractive to Valcoon and she was the same about him.

"Do you know who your new leader will

be?" Valcoon asked.

"There is no next in line. It is a vote. The Shring will find whom they believe will make a great ruler and then that will spread throughout our palace, until one name is the only name, unanimously." She said, adjusting her gloves.

"What about you?! You would make an excellent leader. The way you give speeches and encourage those around you is by my definition, a leader." Valcoon said determined.

"There are no female leaders and never will be. Like I said, it's unanimous." She said coldly.

"So, the dagger you have, is skillfully made. Your race is far more gifted than ours. I've never seen such work before." He mentioned.

"Would you like to see it?" She asked, as she pulled it free.

"May I?!" He said with excitement.

He looked at the craftsmanship of the handle with the Shring head. It was a beauty. There was no flaw in the work. The blade itself was folded only once over and it was extremely sharp. The strength was what puzzled him. He's made blades and swords with Greenite before and he's had to fold it over at least four times to get the durability it needed but with the power of the sun in it has changed the element of the orb.

"It's perfect! How long did it take to craft this?" He asked believing that it had to take several hours or days.

"Our craftsman can make this dagger in less than two hours." She said.

He looked at her like she was mad. If he were to even attempt to remake this dagger, with the same precision, it would take him probably a week and it most likely would be flawed.

"Wow, that's some fucking skills!" He said enthusiastically. "I fancy myself a skilled metal worker, for I made most, if not all the weapons and armor you see, aside from yours and my work is nothing compared to yours." He said, scratching at the space between his horns.

"I know, it shows." She said nonchalantly as she slid her dagger back home.

"Well that was rude!" He said upset.

"I'm being honest. If you want me to lie to you and make you feel good about yourself, then how would you get better at crafting?" She said as she stood up.

She had a point he guessed but damn this female cut deep. Judging someone's work was a slap in the face. "When Viå, Kyö and Sagfrin return, I'll show you my skills!" He said flatly.

"I'd like that." She said.

Elkron came up to the roof after setting up a perimeter around their location and scheduled shift changes. There was nothing for him to write with, so his presence was just that.

Harphrum had figured he wanted answers but said nothing, since it was obvious that there was none. He did however motion for them to go if they wanted. Valcoon accepted the gesture since he was exhausted from the long journey. Harphrum wasn't ready to turn in yet.

Valcoon said goodnight and left Harphrum and Elkron sitting in silence waiting for the return of their allies, or a run in with enemy forces.

Viå had been running at full speed, eating, and drinking what little she had left on the way. She rationed all that she could, and they still had some ways to go. She was tired and wanted to sleep but getting back was more important.

Her run in with the Nightmare was a frightening experience. One she was not ready for and she was glad for the way it turned out. She shivered when she thought about the Nightmare trying to have his way with her. It was terrifying having her clothing torn from her body.

She didn't properly give thanks to Deseri for saving her from a terrible fate. She would make sure she did when she got back.

Taking a break from running, she sat upon a bolder at the foot of a small rock cropping. Sagfrin landed beside her. "So, you found your power?" Sagfrin asked curiously, since they had no time to speak and time was against them, she decided to take this moment.

"I'm not entirely sure yet. It was a different use of my power this time from what I've been doing. It seems that when I focus on different memories that alter my happiness, it alters my powers as well.

"First, I tried what I've been doing when I would take off the collars, but it didn't work, so I focused on the feelings I got from those things that brought raw happiness to me and then it lit up my birthmark." She said, rubbing her finger across it.

"So, you can say that you're getting there." Sagfrin said.

"I'm proud of you Viå. You've been trying forever to use your powers. I'm excited to see what you can do when you've harnessed it completely." Kyö said joining in the conversation.

"I'm just glad, I am able to use it, somewhat." She said. "Are you ready to go now?" She added.

They all took off North.

Tyhim stood looking at his nub as he sat up in bed. He missed it, simply because it was his main hand and using the other was taking time, going used to it. It was a good thing he was skilled with his dagger in both hands, for that was not the problem. It was using it to do other things, simple things.

He went to the corner of the room and pissed in a bucket that was still full of someone's shit; most likely a filthy fucking Molgren. He was more surprised that they would even use one. He leaned over and looked out the window. What he wouldn't give for the sun to be out.

This planet, Ulderelm and before he was born Retula, was always sunny and sometimes cloudy but for the most part sunny. It did rain on occasions and when it did, it came heavy but only for about a week.

Since the purple haze has come, it hasn't done much of anything, except a little rain. It was as if the weather has come to a halt and the little rain was trying to squeeze some life back into it. He noticed that, in order to keep the crops fed with water, the slaves had to do it all manually by carrying massive amounts of water to the fields.

He was no harvester, but he was smart and knew how such things worked. The Shring are a wise race and know many things. They were elusive for sure and for the reason of carrying on their legacy for generations to come but they knew a lot about how things worked.

Tyhim went out to meet with the others. The one, the woman who was supposedly a god, who was going to save this planet had not returned yet.

He was doubtful, she could save it. Watching her fight the Nightmare was a fucking joke. He could have done better if he had his other hand. Knowing now that the daggers can hurt the beast, they didn't need the, "savior" anymore.

He sat beside Jupin and slapped him on the back. Jupin gave him a nod. They had become best friends since leaving the Shring palace. Although the elder was much older, that didn't stop them from obtaining a bond. Both were very much a like; they were always in a foul mood, always popping off with some retort, or usually doing something opposite of the others because their arrogance has overlooked their reason.

"They're back!" Came Valcoon's chattering voice.

Tyhim and Jupin went out with the others. He was now convinced that this was a waste of time and he was going to prove it, the next time they faced the Nightmare.

Viå, Kyö, and Sagfrin, all came to halt before the small group that waited for them outside. Kyö slid himself open and a white light came from inside. Viå reached in a pulled it out.

"Damn, that's a big fucking piece, just for two swords?!" Valcoon said.

"I figured a few more weapons could be made with it. It seems that the white glowing daggers are the strength needed to take out this dark force." Viå said, carrying the Greenite inside the compound.

She laid it down on a table that Valcoon had suggested. He, Vulcil and the other Rharv's started to go to work. A few Shring stayed to watch, interested in the ways of how the Rharv did their metal work and that included Harphrum.

Viå went to find something to nibble on and get some sleep, after she had described how she wanted her swords. Valcoon assured her that he knew what he was doing and that she would be surprised and more than happy by the outcome.

She found some water that tasted like dirt, but she consumed it anyway and the compound had some stock of bread and some vegetables. She went to a room that was available and laid on the stuffed bed. It was uncomfortable, but she had been sleeping in Kyö for years and she vaguely remembers her own bed, so this was actually nice.

She was just about asleep when she heard steps enter the room. She asked mentally to the presence. "Is there an emergency?" She asked, sounding kind of annoyed.

"Just wanting to see, how your trip was." Came Deseri's voice. "But I can return later."

Viå opened her eyes and looked upon the Arglar beauty. Her deep, golden, universe eyes stared at her. "I'm sorry, I'm just tired. I'm actually glad you're here. There was something I needed to say to you." She said, sitting up.

Deseri sat down beside her. Viå felt overwhelmed by her. She thought the feeling would have passed, since they met, and it had until now; now that they were alone.

Deseri looked at her, waiting for her to say what she wanted to say. Viå couldn't quite find the words, feeling the way she did. "I, just wanted to say thank you for saving me. I realized that I never did thank you and I'm sorry."

"You're welcome but you would have done the same. You don't understand how wonderful you are. Coming to a world that isn't yours, to save it. You jumped head first into that beast to protect us all. That took courage. You are a great warrior and should be proud by how skilled you are." Deseri mentioned, flashing Viå a smile.

"I only hope that when I meet him again. I kill him." Viå said coldly.

"I know you will." Deseri confirmed.

"I'm sorry about your friends. You seemed quite upset during their burial." Viå said, feeling like she overstepped Deseri's boundaries.

"It's okay, they'll rest well. Danoka was my partner and I was reflecting our lives together. I will miss her, but I have moved on." She said assuredly.

It was a silly thing that she had not heard one name spoken except Deseri from the Arglar. Was it not custom to call on a name? They did, when they fought, just jumped in like a pack of ferocious animals. They also, when communicating would converse up front with one another. They also had the power to communicate mentally as well.

She also thought it was a little mad to not be upset by losing the one you loved and that one could move on so quickly without any empathy.

"You moved on?" Viå asked curiously, thinking it was rather rash.

"Yes, I find you very interesting and very sexy. You are a strong woman with many mysteries locked behind your eyes. I would like to take the time you have left to know you better. What I'm saying is, I want you as a mate, for the brief duration you have on Ulderelm." Deseri said so boldly without any hesitation.

Viå didn't know what to think, only what

she felt. Though Deseri wasn't human, she did have a human likeness. In reality, Viå wasn't truly human either. She found the creature very attractive and Deseri did do something to her inside that she couldn't explain. In all honesty, Viå had no clue about the being attracted to someone and she had never been in that situation before, since she had been on a mission to save the universe.

Her mother had given her woman advice for when certain woman things happen, and she only touched basis on sexual intercourse, but never had she really thought on it or obviously pursued it.

Viå found herself liking this female. She found her body very appealing and more so her eyes. Maybe the strange feelings she was having was because she liked Deseri.

She didn't think this was the right time for a sexual encounter, her first sexual experience, but then she was indifferent about it. What if she died tomorrow when they went to battle, and she died not know that part of herself. Her mother had told her to, "know yourself completely and only then, will you be happy."

Viå was young and had not really done anything with her life. This was the first real time, that she had done something substantial with it.

She needed to collect herself. This was too fast and unexpected. She had to think. She turned away from the beauty and focused on things, reflecting. Then she turned back to Deseri.

"Listen, you're attractive and I've had these feeling when I first saw you and I'm not sure of what it means but..." She was cut off when Deseri kissed her on the lips.

Taken aback by the sudden kiss, she was lost in thought. Her eyes were wide, staring into those golden eyes. She loved the feeling that ran through her. Fuck it, was all she thought and then she returned the kiss.

The two touched tongues and pressed their lips or lack of lips together. Viå was now on fire. She could not control herself. She was on

Deseri and she accepted. They kissed hard, pressing into one another. Their pelvic areas pressed together, hard. They let go on each other, gave into one another. Each rocked harder against their lower regions.

Deseri pulled off Viå's shirt, exposing her breasts. They touched sensually on one another. Their mouths explored. Deseri kissed Viå's stomach and slid her fingers in the band of her leggings. Viå lifted her rear up off the bed, allowing Deseri to remove them while she still kissed upon her lower stomach.

As Deseri kissed her most private area, Viå went into flames. The fire shot through her entire body. She let herself free from everything in that moment. Nothing around her existed, just the feeling. The two of them let go. Deseri the teacher, Viå the student, both locked into their two worlds, colliding as one.

They laid together cuddled up. The tiny hairs of Deseri were warm against Viå's skin. Viå had not been so relaxed or so comfortable, ever in her entire life. The experience was amazing and life changing. At this moment, she was more than glad she gave in. They dozed off together.

Valcoon was more than pleased on how his work had turned out. He had been up all night, working endlessly on Viå's weapons and he beamed with joy that Harphrum was impressed by his work.

She had been there with him the entire time. At first, she tried to micromanage his work, but he sternly asked her to keep quiet or get out and she kindly stood to the side, observing.

He had taken Viå's existing handles and placed them on the new blades. They were amazing. He found some delicate fabric and made it into a bow on the swords, to offer them as a gift.

The white Greenite was different than what he was used to. It took him a few trials to figure out how it worked but after the sample pieces, he was a pro. He and Elkron stood outside with some of the others, waiting on

Viå, to present his gift.

Time was against them and they wanted to go get her but at the same time didn't want their savior being tired for the battle that was waiting for them. It was a double standard honestly, but she was their only hope.

Sagfrin was done waiting, so she decided to go get her but as soon as she got near the door of the room, it opened to a smiling Viå and a very satisfied Deseri. Sagfrin had a look of, I know what went down in here on her face but mentioned nothing about it. "Viå, we're all ready to march forth and bring down the dark ones. Valcoon has finished with your request as well." She said.

"Thank you Sagfrin. I'm more than ready!" She said cheerfully as she gave Deseri a flirtatious look. Deseri only glared at Sagfrin, still bitter from the abandonment all those years ago.

As they stepped outside, Valcoon had her swords waiting in his hands. She approached and took them from him. She undid the beautiful bow and then tied it up in her hair. She held the swords up, feeling them. They were not as heavy as they once were; no these were not the same, obviously but the balance in them was amazing.

She danced around, swinging them in various ways, feeling their weight and speed. The glow of the swords blurred, leaving a trial of light as they whipped through the air. She slid them into their new home. She grabbed Valcoon's hands and knelt down before him. "Thank you Valcoon for answering my request. They are lovely and precise, and I will use them to save you and everyone else here on Ulderelm!" She said boldly.

Tyhim objected with a spit of disapproval.

"Have I offended you?!" Viå asked him curiously.

He looked at her coldly. "You think that you're going to save us all? Your battle with the Nightmare was pathetic and a clear display of what will come when you face him again if you face him again.

"Anyone of us Shring have more skills than you do and knowing now, what we know to kill him, you are no longer needed! We can do this on our own!" He said cruelly.

Viå looked at him and he was right. They didn't need her. She supposed they never did. A hand touched her back. It was Deseri. She looked at Viå in her hazel eyes and then turned towards Tyhim.

"Step forward and challenge her, fool! If you believe you can take her place, prove it, here and now! Any of you, please step forward if you think she is not needed!" Deseri roared, her voice was eerie but yet still beautiful.

"You don't have to..." Viå said mentally to Deseri but was cut off.

"Yes, I do. He's fucking wrong and has no way of backing his words up!" Deseri retorted as she stared at Tyhim.

"She came here; called forth to save us, to ultimately save the universe from the haze that shrouds us. You think that once you destroy the Nightmare, that you're going to save the universe?! How?! Say how?" She screamed in Tyhim's face.

Tyhim stood, only fuming without any words. He knew the Arglar was right but would not admit that he was weak, especial with one hand. "If I had both my hands, I'd show you!" He said.

"Viå could lose both her hands and still go after the Nightmare and save the universe because that is her duty, her virtue, the reason she is here, the reason she was born. A little thing such as a hand gone is a pathetic excuse for your cowardice!" Deseri vented.

She was egging him on, trying to get him to act on his thoughts, to make him play the fool, but he was actually not mad or unwise. He had no counter to any of what she said. He turned and stalked off.

"That's what I thought!" Deseri called after him.

Viå was beside herself. She was thankful for Deseri standing up for her and she was right, it was her duty but Tyhim was also right, but either way she needed to end the Nightmare and try to bring balance back to this world.

She brought herself back to reality and turned towards Elkron. "Where is the scepter?" She asked him.

"The other elders are watching over it." He answered.

"Please, show me?" She asked and followed him into the compound.

They entered into a large empty room with a table in the center with the scepter laying upon it. Jupin, Framen and Piko all stood around it. They looked up as the two entered the room.

"Ask them if they found anything?" Elkron asked Viå.

"Did you find anything, yet?" She asked.

"Nothing. It can't be analyzed. As far as we're concerned it's just a wooden rod with a round stone in it." Jupin stated. Viå relayed the information to Elkron.

He approached it and tried his luck and got nothing. The door opened and Sagfrin came in and stood next to Viå. "Are they analyzing it?" She asked.

Viå nodded. "But they can't find anything. It looks like a simple stick and stone." She said.

Sagfrin did the same as Elkron and got the same results. "I wonder how it works, if it can't be analyzed? Where does the power come from?" She asked, confused.

"Sagfrin, pick it up please." Viå asked. Sagfrin nervously scooped it up and slid it off the table, catching it with her foot. "Now, I want you to use it." Viå said. Sagfrin gave her a puzzled look. "Try it on that window." She said pointing.

Sagfrin pointed the scepter at the window and nothing. "Focus." Viå said. Sagfrin tried again and nothing. Viå had all the elders do it and nothing. Viå picked it up and only pointed it, blowing out the window along with the frame.

A group of beings came running, looking inside at the six of them. Viå stepped through the hole and handed it Valcoon who had showed up to see what the fuse was. Viå ordered him to use it. Still nothing. She gave it to Deseri and nothing. In the back watching was Harphrum. Viå asked her if she would like to try.

Harphrum came over and took it from Deseri. She focused it on a rubble of rocks out in the distance, but nothing happened. Viå retrieved the scepter and pointed it towards the rubble and blew the pile away, leaving nothing but a bare spot after the dust settled. She tapped her fingers on the shaft, thinking.

"Is the Nightmare a god?" She asked to anyone who could answer.

"I don't believe so. As far as we know he's just a creation, to be like a god." Elkron answered.

Viå was more than confused. Why couldn't anyone else use the scepter of tribulation? The story she was told of it once being a god, only added to the confusion. If it was once a god, then how come it could not turn back into what it once was?

She held it in front of herself and did what she did with the collars and Dianna. She felt it, opened it and with her powers, she found the darkness within.

It was unlike anything she had felt before. It was alive. It had the living parts of life. She reached for a conscience and it was there. She spoke to it. "Hello?" But it didn't answer. "I can feel you. You can trust in me." She said, but it remained silent, then suddenly a loud voice came into her mind. "Please! Help! I'm a slave to my own creation!" The voice shouted.

"Who are you?" She asked.

"I'm nothing but who I am! Please, use the light that courses through your veins and set me free!" It screamed.

She came into her own, puzzled over this god within the scepter, it somehow knew of her powers. Was it truly as it was rumored? Why go through the lengths of transforming one's self, just to be destroyed? She thought on it for a moment then decided to make a deal. "Would you be willing to help me and in return I'll help you?" She asked.

"I want this suffering to end. I've been trying to free myself for ages. It was a selfish mistake on my part to think I could elude death and imprisonment, to only do just that. What is it you request?" It asked.

"I need your strength to end this battle and then I will set you free." She said.

"One last time?" The god asked.

"I promise, one last time." Viå confirmed.

The Plea

They marched on through the dusty terrain. Each had their fill of food and drink. For some it would be their last.

Viå was still in euphoria from her encounter with Deseri but she was still also upset by Tyhim's words. She told herself to let it go and focus on why she was here but that really didn't seem to help.

The Shring continued to spar with each other, keeping their skills sharp. They were very well rounded in combat and they could probably hold their own against the Nightmare. The one thing Viå had overall was her tenacity to complete what she has set out to do. She doubted that any of them had her drive. None of this moving forward would have not happened if she had not shown up. They've all been in hiding and enslaved since her arrival and now most are free.

Sagfrin landed next to Viå, who hasn't really said much since she was united back with Elkron. The two had for the most part been inseparable. "How are you holding up?" Sagfrin asked.

"I'm doing pretty well considering." Viå answered, looking at her friend.

"Don't listen to that Shring. They've been hiding their whole lives and are doing this for their own gain." Sagfrin mentioned.

"I know but it still cut pretty deep. It was an overwhelming moment and I've placed it away for now. It was hard hearing half-truths, but I've got a mission and I aim to fulfill it." Viå said.

"I'm glad it didn't deter you from your chosen path. Any one of us would have left or given up. We don't have the mind set you do to see things through. We ran when all of this started, when we should have fought but that has passed, and we can only hope that we can be forgiven through this battle." Sagfrin said, looking ashamed.

"You're here now and that is what matters. Your transgressions were forgiven when you joined the fight." Viå said encouraging her friend.

"Thank you Viå, you truly are a great friend." She said and flew off back towards Elkron.

The Nightmare sat in his throne with a pile of dead naked woman at his feet. He hasn't stopped feeding and fucking since his return. He was on edge that he was most likely going to lose this battle.

He was confused by this woman who has come to challenge him. She was not created by his brother. She was something else entirely. That shooting star must have been this woman, it only made sense. Was she a creation of the gods? He was in a mental confusion.

As he sucked the blood from another woman, his wound was itching. The light dagger that cut him had created a flesh wound, an irritating flesh wound. Since his skin was impenetrable except by his own teeth and obvious the light daggers, he could not stitch the wound.

It seems his brothers creations had found a way to best him after all. What baffled him most, was that the Shring, his brother created from the last game had managed to allude them upon creating the new one, just as did the blood pixies.

He wished he would have thought of the alternatives to this creation he was trapped inside of. It seemed like his brother always knew what he was planning, since he countered everything. He put that aside and focused on the dilemma at hand. He was going to need to kill this woman most likely sent by the gods and then everything else to get back to the other side.

The threat should be arriving anytime, and

he was going to go out and meet them. She had his scepter though and that was a bigger problem. The power in a single swing can destroy everything. When used on a living being, it could only hold them, not blast them into pieces but that didn't mean she couldn't bring the palace down on top of them.

When he had found the scepter, he and his brother had only just begun the new game. It was a very clear starry night, as it always was before the darkness arrived. He was putting his own position into power, with the help of the Molgren's. People who he had turned into beasts by a creation of his own, known as the Hand.

The Hand, like the Shadow was a single being who he had created to help with his chances to overturn his brother's creations. The Hand got greedy and tried to rule on his own but was challenged by the leader of the people. The Hand lost but not before placing the curse the Nightmare had originally sent him out to do. In a way the Hand succeeded but the Nightmare lost a powerful ally in the process.

After he had the Molgren's under his rule, he was putting the strongest ones into positions of power to suit his war, when an object fell from the sky. He flew to where it had fallen and in a compression from the force of impact laid the scepter.

He picked it up and looked at it and felt the god within. He spoke to it and it told him its story. The Nightmare used his powers to seal the god inside forever, which gave power to the scepter. He waved it around and started tearing the world apart. He gave it a suitable name for the damage it could do; the scepter of tribulation. It's been with him ever since.

He looked down from the hole he had created when he smashed through the doors and the hall wall to see if his enemies had arrived. Why he didn't use the giant hole he made using the scepter when he cleaned the throne room from the pile of Molgren's that littered it was because he didn't give a fuck.

He could see the throng of his oppressors out in the distance. They would arrive soon but not for a couple hours. Down below his forces had formed ranks. They were many; Molgren's mixed with the dead. His forces out numbered theirs by at least a hundred to one. He knew that was nothing with the scepter in their possession.

He had not seen or heard from his blood pixies since they brought in the elder. He wondered if they had somehow been destroyed and wondered who could have done so. That woman perhaps but she was no match for him, so he couldn't see how that could be.

He wondered if his brother was watching from the other side, from the veil of the gods but then again, if he was losing his god powers, perhaps so was his brother. Only once he finished this game would he know for sure and finish it he would.

They still had a long way to go but even from their distance the tower of Drenchin was unbelievably high. The gates of the city were massive and the walls that went around Drenchin traveled what looked like miles to the East and West.

The inside must be expansive, Viå thought. She was tired, irritated, and filthy. Once this was over, if she succeeds, she was going to take a long soothing bath. She was sure they all would.

They marched on in no real order. They were mixed up together. She figured they were just going to wing it, since none of them ever spoke of a strategy. Why put someone in a situation they were uncomfortable in, when someone who wants to strive in any situation, can? It was pretty clear they were all here to fight for their home, so just go for it, head first.

As they got closer, the dark shadow of the Nightmare descended down beyond the gates, behind his forces. He stood brooding beyond his multitude of dark ones.

Viå had no intentions of fighting the dead. They didn't choose to be here, so why not give them their peace. She felt her connection to her power, to the light inside of her. Her empathy for the dead had brought it forth. She grasped it within and held on to it as she had done with the darkness.

Since her powers were new to her, she had only scratched the surface. She could feel a much deeper and more powerful connection to her birthmark. She spoke to Sagfrin, Elkron, Deseri, Valcoon and Harphrum mentally, asking them if they had a plan and they all confirmed her own thoughts. Nope.

"Kyö, how are you holding up?" Viå asked her old friend.

"I'm doing good. Ready to help save Ulderelm!" He said excitedly.

"I'm glad because it's about to begin!" She stated.

The Shadow stood out front of the dead, which was fitting, since looked like he belonged. He held up his new hand that he had ripped off, one of the dead and it was perfect. He dropped it forward, pointing towards the approaching throng. Out from within the resurrected, came the dead children, some holding infants. They marched out to meet their enemy.

Once they had arrived in the city, the Shadow had equipped the resurrected with weapons. The ones who could hold them. He neglected to have them practice since they were dead, and any fool can swing a weapon, plus they were many and should have no trouble killing the small group.

The Shadow smiled, almost laughed as he pictured the faces of his enemies once they seen the children. He wished that he was standing right there when they came out and started walking towards them. A priceless display of, "what the fuck?"

He waited for the children to reach the elders group before sending out the horde of resurrected. He wanted to see what the kids could do.

Viå and Sagfrin shared a look as they

watched dead children coming at them. They were in an awkward situation. None of them wanted to hurt children. Viå decided to try her powers, the one she has been clutching upon. She stepped out in front of her warriors.

She felt her connection with her birthmark. It was intimate. The circle with the crescent in its center lit up in its aqua-green. She held her arm out towards the children. The birthmark engulfed her hand in an aqua-green fire ball. She focused on it, concentrating on what she wanted to accomplish. The ball of light grew brighter and brighter. So much energy was coming forth from her.

As the children got closer, they didn't stop from the light. The ones who touched the edges of the aqua-green light, fell back into their restful state.

She released the power. It took off, shrouding all the kids, hitting them like a wave. They toppled to the ground, back to their forever sleep. The light continued onward and disappeared midway between their group and the Nightmare's forces.

"Doubting her still?" Harphrum asked Tyhim, who didn't answer and remained skeptical.

"Let's go!" Viå screamed, holding the scepter over her head and started running towards the Nightmare's first line of defense.

Everyone shouted as they ran, following Viå to try and end the war.

"That woman has great powers; like a god. Who is she and why is she here? She's interfering with a game that none have any idea they are playing! If she is a god, then she could most likely kill me, kill me!" The Nightmare said to himself.

The fear of actually dying was starting to rise in him. He needed to figure out the strategy when he comes face to face with this woman. Should he consult with her? No that would be cowardice but then again this was just a game and all he really wanted was to get out of this shell.

One thing remained on his mind. How come she still possessed powers? Could she see the veil? He needed answers and ultimately, he would do anything for them.

He was for now the ruler of Ulderelm and could stop all this right now, but his character demanded blood and fornication to thrive. Maybe he should give in. In case this escaladed to his untimely death.

He honestly expected to win this game, but this new player was real, and it was a chance he couldn't take. He stepped forward and screamed a loud, terrifying scream that sent chills to the core. The throng stopped before the battle had even started.

Viå paused when the scream cut through the noise of the shouting forces in motion. He walked through his own forces, not caring who was in his way. He opened his wings and cleared a wider path, tossing his own forces through the air.

Viå summoned the power and harnessed it,

building it, waiting for the Nightmare to come closer so she could catch his darkness. He held up his hands and slowly kept waking at her and stopped. She glared, waiting for him to make his move.

"May we talk civilized?" He asked in his deep growling voice.

She spoke to him mentally, not trusting this mad tactic. "What is it that you wish to speak about?" She asked still waiting for his attack.

"Where is it you come from?" He asked.

"Why?" She asked.

"I ask because you have the powers of a god but, yet you walk among mortals." He stated curiously to her mind.

"I was born in a place called Buriece and I walk among mortals because I am like them, but I also happen to be part god." She said, still on edge that he would attack at any moment.

"How is this that you are part god but have powers only a true god possesses?" He questioned.

"My grandmother broke her bond with her sisters, falling in love with one of her own creations. She became pregnant and had my mother and then my mother had me. How I have these powers are unknown, but I do possess them." She said.

"Interesting." He said looking off in the distance. "How is it that your powers still work with the darkness?" He asked.

She looked at him for a long drawn out moment. "I was informed that you are not a god." She said.

"You know the rules of how the world of the gods work. The created can't be interfered with, so obviously they know nothing but what they see." He said.

"I'm confused. This is not you?" She said pointing at him.

"Many years ago, the sole creator birthed us here as any other place and we, like other gods started to build our own world and instead of creating a world, we created several. It is a game that my brother Shalg and I play. We create the players and we let them go to war against one another and so on, then we start over. This game has lasted the longest of all the games, due to my imprisonment as this. Now this purple haze of darkness has polluted our world which has caused some beneficial factors in the game but also hindered my use of god powers.

"You see, I created this shell as a way to put myself in the playing field, so I could try and beat my brother but there were complications and now I'm trapped.

"I stopped this fight when I figured out that you must be a god, because you could ultimately kill me, and I needed you to know that this isn't real; it's just a game." He said, trying to sound innocent.

"Not real? A game? I've been here in Ulderelm for some time and have put myself through trials for the survival of these creatures. I have had meals, conversations and some very intimate moments with all of these creatures and I can tell you, they are very much real.

"I get that you gods do things for your own selfish needs, but these are real, living, breathing creations. I am part of them and part of the gods and you and your brother are wicked. Creating things that believe they have a purpose but then are removed and replaced by another world, another game! Tell me why I shouldn't kill you for your devious ways?!" She screamed in anger.

"You think this is the only place where gods are not playing games with their creations? Every god is playing a game. The sole creator is playing a fucking game, but on a much larger scale and you're trying to justify my actions!" He said, trying to defend himself.

"It's not fair to fuck with the lives of the living! Why should you get to make the decisions of their destiny?" She fumed.

"Obsolete, they are, we all are. Why do you care? It's not even your home. You can't change the universe that you were born of?" He mentioned, still being an ass.

"So, what do you expect to gain from telling me this? What is the point?" She asked, curiously.

"To not kill me. To know this is just a game and to not take it seriously. I needed to warn you in case you actually did kill me, because it would be a mistake to kill a god. I was also wanting to know if you can see the other side?" He asked.

She looked at him very confused. Her mother had never mentioned another side in her messages. "I'm not sure what you mean?"

"The world of the gods that looks into this side. A god can see into it. I'm sure the darkness has separated both worlds. Do you think you can call forth my brother or return me to that world?" He asked almost begging.

"How?" She questioned.

"You possess great powers still and are not plagued by the darkness and I'm sure you can contact him or maybe bring the veil into view." He answered.

Viå turned away from the Nightmare. She

had him beat. He was frightened of death yet could kill an entire planet of individual personalities without even blinking.

She looked at all the faces. All of them wishing they could hear their conversation. All of them wanting answers. All of them wondering what was happening. Her heart burned, thinking about the suffering all of these beings have went through and soon they would all be destroyed, and a new group would take their place.

Tears filled her eyes. This couldn't go on any longer. These gods are selfish and would not change, given the chance. Their superior minds could not allow them to share in the equality of a lesser creation. She knew what she had to do. She found her calling and it was much greater than just curing the universe of the haze.

It was bringing justice to the universe. She probably could unite the two brothers but that would mean she would have to take on two gods at once and that was not going to happen.

She turned and face the god.

"Fuck yourself!" She shouted for all to hear and released her powers. The aqua-green light turned into a beam from the rage she felt inside and pierced a hole through the Nightmare's chest. His arms went out to the sides and his head tipped up towards the sky.

All the power of her light entered into the Nightmare and blazed from his mouth, eyes and nose and then he burst into pieces.

His outer shell exploded sending blood, guts, and flesh everywhere. His god body was free from the Nightmare but not free from Viå's powers. His original body lit up, burning bright to the point that she couldn't see what he actually looked like. Everyone turned away from the blinding light, except Viå. She needed to make sure this god was done. Its body shattered, bursting into what looked like tiny pieces of glass and fell to the ground.

She waved the scepter of tribulation and pulled all the dark ones to the ground and with her powers, locked them there and placed a part of herself within the scepter and shoved it in the ground, vertically. The power she infused with the scepter, made it so she didn't need to hold it, to do what she wanted.

"Let it be known that right now, you are a free world and there will be only the laws you all set in place. You will no longer be ruled by god's but by your own selves!" She ignited her powers and placed them inside of all the dark ones. She felt the darkness within coursing through their blood and severed it with her pure, calming, loving thoughts.

The dead went limp and were now at peace forever and the Molgren's, she had turned back into their human forms, where they would no longer be hindered by the light.

The Shadow was something else entirely and she knew that he couldn't go free. He was made for one thing and that was to take life and as far as she could tell from the darkness within him that he had no glimmer of light at all. She knelt down beside his bone skull.

I would set you free, but you lack the power

to change. You were made to destroy and there is no alternative for you, so I say goodbye." She placed a hand on his skull and with the light, replaced the darkness. He begged and screamed until his skull turned dry and began to crack, then it started chipping away, until it went flat, crushing and turning into dust. The smoke cloak evaporated into the air.

She returned to the scepter and pulled it free and released the throng from their hold. The humans who had once been Molgren's, were confused by their whereabouts. It seems that when they were transformed, their memory was too.

She closed her eyes and homed in on the brother, the other god and his whereabouts. She had found him, sitting, and waiting. He looked lost. He turned in her direction. He could feel her but obviously he could not see her. She opened her eyes and looked upon all the faces.

"Is it finished?" Elkron asked.

"Not yet. I have a few more things I need to

do." She said and walked over and touched Sagfrin's face. "Ulderelm is now yours to do with what you will. Just know that the gods of this world will no longer exist. My suggestion is to make peace and live out the rest of your days in happiness. I must go but I'll return to say goodbye." Sagfrin had tears rolling down her face. She was so happy to be done with the chaos.

Viå turned to Deseri and told her that she must go and that she'll return. The Arglar nodded.

Viå jumped inside Kyö and off towards the North they went.

Birthright

U p North in the mountains was where she had seen the other god, dwelling. She has now sworn to herself that she is making it her duty to kill all of them. It wasn't fair that they could meddle with the lives of those they create. She understood why they did it but that didn't make it right.

She came to Ulderelm to balance out the darkness but in doing so she had gained friendships and those were worth more in the end and she wasn't going to stand for these gods playing games. Fuck that.

Her mission has changed and for good reason and this brother was going to suffer the same fate as the other.

Why the god perched himself up so high

was probably the same reason the god's played games, because they were the dominant beings, but not for long.

She didn't care what this god was going to say. She was going to use her power or run a sword through him. It all made sense now. She had found her birthright, her purpose. It wasn't to settle down or to be a slave. It was this. Find gods and end their tyranny on those created.

She was no longer lost, confused, scared or empty. No, she was happy, excited and above all; delighted to have found her purpose.

She climbed out of Kyö at the point where the gods presence was strongest. The snow was up to her thighs and cold. This was a first for her. She picked some up for no other reason but to touch it, feel it, have an experience. She didn't know when the next the chance, if ever, would be.

She let it fall out her hands and focused on why she had travelled all this way. The other side was losing its powers and now facing a conundrum and it was the perfect time for her to make her move.

Though she promised to release the god within the scepter, she now changed her mind, which made her smile because she was contradicting her new-found purpose. It was another selfish god and she was aimed on killing two gods at once.

Yes, two at once but not brothers at once, bent on revenge. Her plan was simple. Get close enough and stab the god in his heart with the scepter. Was it that simple? She was going to try.

Did she have the power to see into the world of god's? She must if she was able to scurry the whereabouts of the brother. Could she travel there? She was part god. She wondered if her mother could travel between parallels. Her mother had tried to tell her everything that she may need to know, but this alternate void was not something she mentioned. She guessed it had to do with the fact that; of course, gods came from somewhere else, since you could not see them. She felt naive a lot on this journey, but she was finding herself and that was the number one thing her mother wanted her to do. So being ignorant and naive were a part of that and so she accepted it.

She reached the light within and put her mental hands around it, pressing in on it, compressing the energy. For this to work, she was going to need to actually dispel the darkness from Ulderelm, she was going to need to bring the power of the god's back from their dormant state and that was going to require a massive amount of energy. Energy and power; she didn't know if she had it, but she was going to try.

She stabbed the scepter into the snow and pulled her swords free. She was going to need assistance and the power of the sun trapped within the Greenite of her blades, should boost her powers.

She ignited the light outwards into her swords, placing her powers into them and then she pulled from it. The power within from the sun was strong, so strong that she could have used a single sword to do the work she was about to do. How she just knew what needed done alluded her, it was as if she was doing it by instinct, as if she had been doing it her whole life.

The mental hands pressing in on the power was super charging her pure light. The birthmark was white hot, sparking and crackling, ready to release. She held it a little longer. She wasn't exactly sure how much power was needed, only that it was a lot.

She opened herself up like the flowers she remembered from Buriece. With a smile on her face, everything she loved was in that moment, in that power. The release was smooth and went forth out into the darkness, cutting it, severing it. Her power replaced the purple mass that clouded Ulderelm and its surrounding attributes, such as the sun and two moons.

The sun beamed down upon her and the

whole surface of Ulderelm. It was such beauty and refreshing. She could see the valley below, all lit up. The beings of this world had a lot of work ahead of them, to restore the order but they will live free after she kills this brother, this god.

"Who are you?" A voice came from behind her. She turned and standing on the other side of an iridescent green light that wavered, like a wall of water was the god, the brother. He was tall and strange looking. His eyes were hollow, and he was without a mouth or nose. His body, if she had to guess was a light orange but the wavering wall made it hard to tell.

Whether he looked like the former brother was unknown, since his body was lit up like a white-hot blaze and was gone before she could make sense of what she was seeing and now he was scattered at the gates of Drenchin.

"I am Viå and this is Kyö. I am the goddess sent here to dispel the darkness that was polluting Ulderelm." She stated.

He looked at her with a very awkward silence. "I gathered that you had succeeded in saving Ulderelm. Are the elders okay, did they make it? When the darkness came, it hindered my powers, so I could no longer see into that world. The last of my strength was used upon the summoning of me by the elders.

"I had a council with a few gods and the sole creator had said that he would send help and he didn't fail." The brother said.

"The elders made it and the Nightmare, and his dark ones have been defeated." She said.

"My brother should be here by now, I've been out of contact with him even before the darkness intruded. He always arrives after I prove my greatness."

"Your brother was trapped within the Nightmare." She said flatly, waiting to see his reaction.

He stood looking at her with his empty eyes. It was interesting not being able to discern his face from the lack of a mouth or nose. "I see. A fool he was then. Meddling in a war that was not meant for him to physically partake. Was it peaceful?" He asked.

"Unpleasant, for I condemned him for his atrocious ways of deceiving the life you and he created. Using them in your own selfish game just to see who the more dominating god is. He suffered greatly." She said coldly, trying to invoke the god.

"You killed him, intentionally?" He asked. His voice sounded disheartened.

"I did. He asked if I would help him get back to the other side, to you and I denied his request." She stated.

She had no idea about this veil, but she was sure she could not pass through it, but could he? She stood her ground. She knew that she had touched a sore spot and she had her plan in motion.

Though she restored the balance to this world, she believed that this god was still weak; She hoped.

"A hand grabbed her neck from behind and shoved her forward, holding her up against the iridescent wall. The god still stood on the other side. He leaned down and put his face close to hers. "You are going to suffer!" The gods voice said from behind her.

How was this possible? The god in two places at once? This was not her plan and now she had to improvise. Frightened, she reached for her power, but it was useless for she could not clear her mind enough from the overwhelming situation she was in.

She tried to stab the god, but he caught her hand and squeezed, crushing it. She screamed out in pain as bones snapped and shattered beneath her skin. Her sword fell to the ground. She started to cry from the pain. She tried to swing on him with her other sword, but it was no good.

Viå fell to her knees as the grip on her neck released. She looked at the cause and it was Kyö, forcing himself at the god but now the god had his arms around Kyö and began squeezing, trying to crush him.

Through the blurry vision of the tears in her

eyes, she now had her opportunity to follow through with her plan. She slid the sword she was holding back home and then picked up the other and did the same. She held her broken hand against her chest as she rushed to retrieve the scepter of tribulation. In a flash, she picked it up and, in a blur, rushed towards the god. She jumped into the air over Kyö and planted both feet into the gods face.

The force rocked his head back as she landed on her butt on top of Kyö and then she quickly pushed off, soaring through the air with the end of scepter facing outward, like a dagger. It pushed right into the gods flesh and hopefully into his heart. She dropped to the ground.

The god looked down and then back at Viå. He smiled and went to grab the rod but was stopped mid motion. The power of Viå was still imprinted inside of the scepter, which gave her hands-free control.

She found the power inside but was losing it. Her anger and her fear, not to mention the pain was messing with her. The god could not move but could he use the powers he had? She closed her eyes and slowly breathed. She thought about Kyö and the times they shared. She envisioned Sagfrin's face and Deseri's and thought of their time spent together and the bonds they made. She looked at the Rharv, Valcoon and how beautiful his skills were in crafting such magnificent swords.

The emotions of all her friends and the joy they brought her and the suffering they endured touched her core. She lit up brighter than ever before. She feared nothing, she felt no pain, only herself, who she was as an individual and what she stood for and that was freedom. The freedom to live happy without the injustice of being controlled, enslaved, without the fear of what comes next. No one should have to suffer, and these gods were the shackles but not anymore.

"Your kind. The havoc of god's is no more!" She said with conviction and placed her hand on the scepter. It lit up like a flame. The power she released was so strong that when it entered the rod it started splitting down the shaft. Beams of white hot light broke free into the god. His black sockets looked at her with a bunched-up brow line. Suddenly the empty sockets shot out light into the sky.

The god made no sound as it's skin broke open from the power. He like his brother, along with the scepter of tribulation shattered into billions of tiny fragments that sparkled like glass and then dropped to the snow, leaving little impressions.

She looked at her best friend. "He didn't hurt you, did he?" She asked.

"Only when he broke your hand." He said.

Once she was reminded, the pain came throbbing back to life. She pulled it close to herself again. "Thanks for saving me bestie!" She said and put her face on him. "I love you Kyö!"

"I love you too... bestie."

Farewell Ulderelm

When her and Kyö got back to Drenchin, everyone was still gathered in and outside of the gates. Her and Kyö approached the throng. Everyone was in good spirit. The five elders, Valcoon, Harphrum, and Deseri came out to meet them.

"So, did you take care of what you needed?" Deseri asked.

Viå nodded. "It is done. You will rule yourselves. There will be no gods to control your lives."

"Where will you go from here?" Sagfrin asked.

"I'm going home but not before I keep the promise I made to myself and the universe." She said. "But first!" Viå reached out and touched Sagfrin on her face and put light into her and then moved on to Elkron, Jupin, Piko and finally Framen.

"That should keep your wings free from the dirt." She said smiling.

Each elder spoke aloud for the first time after all the years of being silent. They were all crying, thankful to finally be able to communicate. Each thanked her with a bow.

Deseri came close and wrapped her arms around Viå, pulling her in tight. The Arglar looked into her eyes and then gave Viå a hard, passionate kiss and then grabbed her butt. "A memory for you and one for me. I will never forget you Viå the goddess, warrior of freedom. Safe travels my friend." Deseri said.

Viå beamed brightly. "I will, and I'll never forget you. I'll think of you all often. Thank you for helping me and enjoy your new lives and don't take things for granted." She stuck a fist out towards Valcoon. He turned his head to the side, confused.

She grabbed his hand and folded it like hers

and then bumped it. "Something from my home, that I just remembered. It means friendship and respect." She said, as he stood looking at his fisted hand and then have Viå a bright smile.

A healer approached and asked to heal her hand, she gladly accepted. She moved and flexed her fingers in her hand, the pain was gone.

"Thank you Viå for returning our world back to it's sunny, chaos free self. You will never be forgotten." Elkron said.

Everyone took that day to celebrate the new world. Getting it back in order was going to have to wait. Viå would have liked to stay but she had many years to travel and a mission to fulfill. They said their final farewells and Viå climbed inside Kyö and off they went, she waved as they ascended into the sky.

"Where to?" Kyö asked.

"To kill the one god! Do you know where

he dwells?" She asked.

"No but there are plenty of stops along the way and I'm sure someone knows!" He said and off they went.

Made in the USA
Monee, IL
02 September 2019